FALLEN FOR A LIE

CONNOR WHITELEY

No part of this book may be reproduced in any form or by any electronic or mechanical means. Including information storage, and retrieval systems, without written permission from the author except for the use of brief quotations in a book review.

This book is NOT legal, professional, medical, financial or any type of official advice.

Any questions about the book, rights licensing, or to contact the author, please email connorwhiteley@connorwhiteley.net

Copyright © 2023 CONNOR WHITELEY

All rights reserved.

DEDICATION

Thank you to all my readers without you I couldn't do what I love.

CHAPTER 1
16th September 2022
London, England

Intelligence Officer Jamie Owen knelt down on a bright pink gardening-kneeing-pad on the wonderfully warm cobblestone path in the middle of London's largest community green space. Jamie had always liked donating some of his time to this special place. A place that bought so much happiness to families, young couples and elderly people just wanting somewhere calm to relax in their older age.

A very large bed of untidy pink roses were in front of him then another bed of yellow roses with some red and blue and white flowers were also thrown in there to help give the park some kind of patriotic British rubbish. Jamie wasn't a fan of that bed of plants in the slightest but thankfully there were so many (and sometimes so few volunteers) that he never had any reason to deal with it.

Jamie loved the wonderful hints of lavender, pine

and lilacs that reminded him of freshly roasted crispy lamb from family dinners in the garden from when he was a child, as a gentle early autumn breeze blew past that made him cheeks warm up for a moment before the breeze stopped.

A lot of his intelligence friends had asked Jamie why he bothered donating his time here when he could have enjoyed the finer things in life given where he worked. But Jamie had always just shook his head at his friends when they said silly things like that.

Jamie giving his time to the local green spaces wasn't about enjoying fine things. It was about helping London to be a better place without any espionage actions. Jamie loved creating and maintaining and protecting these green spaces so everyone could have a place to come and relax. Something that was even more important considering almost everyone in London didn't have a garden and only had a little apartment to themselves.

Jamie focused a little more on all the bright pink roses in front of him and they were all beautiful. They were so full of life, strong and they were looked like they could deal with anything. Jamie almost smiled that the similarities to himself, he liked adventure and surviving in the wild, much like these roses did.

And roses always had thorns on them to protect themselves, another trait Jamie loved about them.

The delightful sound of young families laughing and talking and children playing behind him as they ran up and down the cobblestone path like they were possessed. But Jamie loved seeing everyone happy, that was probably another reason why he loved doing this so much.

After spending so much time as a Division Agent, seeing the worse in humanity and sometimes just getting flat out depressed at what humans were capable of, it was so refreshing to see how happy and amazing normal people could be.

Jamie reached into the bed of roses and started to pick out some of the dead leaves that were hiding under the bright pink rose heads. No one could probably see them but Jamie just wanted to do a little bit of work today.

"You know sweetheart," a woman said behind him. "I'm all for gays but you do make it difficult when you're surrounded by bright pink roses,"

Jamie just smiled as he heard the voice of his best friend, mentor and fellow Division agent, Maura Ratliff. Jamie loved working in Division with her, the top-secret and semi-autonomous division of MI5 and the British Government that allowed them to investigate things without having to ask permission.

Jamie loved that concept alone, and it was so much better than working with MI5 directly, like he had for a decade before Maura found him for Division.

Jamie brushed his hands on his worker's trousers, got up and hugged Maura. She might have been as thin as a rake but she always gave the best hugs in the entire world.

And even today, which was technically a day off for everyone in Division, she still looked great with her white blouse, black trousers and black high heels. That Jamie knew certainly contained a small knife and a pistol.

Jamie was about to start explaining what he was doing here to try and get Maura interested. But the way she was dressed, the half-loving, half-serious expression on her beautiful face and just the way that she was composing herself.

His day-off was over and Jamie was excited about it.

"How bad?" Jamie asked.

Maura gave Jamie an evil smile. "Ready for your first ever Code Black mission?"

Jamie smiled, his stomach filled with butterflies and he was a lot more terrified than he ever wanted to admit. Code Black missions were the worse of the worse, it was something that was so apocalyptic that it was an all-hands-on-deck mission.

This was beyond bad.

But Jamie couldn't work out why this was a Division case. Normally MI5 and MI6 sorted out these cases depending on whether it was to do with national or international security and who had jurisdiction it was, Division never got Code Black Cases.

So why was Division getting it?

The answer to that had Jamie more than concerned than he wanted to admit. But whatever happened this was going to be the start of an amazing day.

And he couldn't wait in the slightest.

CHAPTER 2
16th September 2022
London, England

Psychologist Doctor Luca Kelly sat at his very modern brown oak desk in a bright white little office with a stunning view over the amazing city of London. Luca had a large pile of folders open as he tried to memorise the guest list for tonight but right now he was simply enjoying the little view out of his stunning window.

Luca had always liked London because it was honestly rather amazing with its such diverse range of culture, influences and amazing areas. His personal favourite just had to be Soho, mainly for all the gay bars and clubs and other wonderful delights. But it was just a shame that his job stopped him from enjoying the city as much as he once did.

Luca had really liked growing up in England so close to London. It was only a quick half hour train ride away. It meant he didn't have to put up with all the ugly London traffic and ridiculously high prices, but at the weekend (and some school nights when he was annoyed at his parents) he could simply jump on a train, go to gay clubs and be back by early morning.

It was the perfect life for a teenager really.

Luca liked the sensational smell of freshly ground bitter coffee that filtered through his large office door as his fellow psychologists finished up their work for tonight. And Luca partly wished that he was just going home tonight anyway to his big empty flat with his cats. Granted his mum and sister were staying with him for the week and that was just another reason not to go home.

Luca really loved them both and it was really kind of them to travel down from Edinburgh Scotland to see him. Yet he didn't really want another night of *when are you getting a boyfriend, when am I having grandchildren* and *when are you going to get a real job.*

Luca had absolutely no idea which of those questions he hated more. He was currently in-between boyfriends at the moment since the last one... well cheated on him. He would happily have children with his boyfriend when he actually had one, and psychology was a real job.

He didn't see clients every single day of the week (except Saturdays as he played poker that day) that suffered from depression to anxiety to post-traumatic stress disorder for the fun of it. He did it because he wanted to help these amazing people improve their lives and alleviate their psychological distress.

Luca's computer beeped as another email came through, and that really made Luca smile.

It was from his best friend, Alice Zelly, and current leader of the Scottish Government's political party in Westminster (the heart of the UK Government) saying that she would like to have him there tonight at some big political function.

Luca still loved it that after him and his family had grown fed-up of all the corruption, cronyism and other utter rubbish that went on in Westminster. They had moved to Scotland, fell in love with the country and really wanted it to gain its freedom from the corrupt UK Government.

So when he ran into a young woman working with the Scottish Government a few years ago and helped her with her depression. They had become fast friends and when Luca had moved back to London for some work, she had found him and offered him a little temp work on behalf of the Scottish Government.

Luca was hardly going to say no.

Granted Luca had no real clue what the party was about tonight. He had only emailed Alice because she had mentioned the party in passing and something about it was the perfect opportunity to help convince the UK Government officials of the democratic right of the Scottish to choose their own path in life.

Of course Luca absolutely knew it was useless going to the party for that reason because no members of the UK Government would ever listen to a so-called crazy Scot. But Luca would never say no to a great party filled with hot young men in tight tailored suits and even though this was a government party, and the government hated gays, there was at least a small chance there would be another gay there to talk to.

And hopefully do something more with.

With the sun slowly starting to set over London and the sky becoming veiled by the fiery orange of the setting sun, Luca just smiled, closed his laptop and really wanted to get home quickly so he could get changed into something a little more attractive for the party.

He was of course going to support his real Government first (at least that's what he would tell Alice) but if he found a beautiful guy to talk to he wasn't going to pass up such a great opportunity.

CHAPTER 3
16th September 2022
London, England

Jamie stepped into the very top-secret large box-room that served as Division's headquarters in the very heart of London. Jamie had never really been a fan of its jet black walls that stretched for tens of metres to create a perfect square that was electronically shielded from the rest of the world so no one could ever spy on them.

Jamie had always enjoyed seeing the bright faces of new recruits enter the headquarters expecting to see so much cool technology, computers and gadgets. And then only to see their faces drop in confusion as they realised the reality of Division.

The only technology in the entire headquarters was a massive TV screen attached to the very end wall so everyone could see a mission unfolding together, a long row of computers on brown desks and a small gadget cabinet below the TV screen. It was a great amount of technology but for some reason new recruits were always disappointed.

Jamie had been disappointed too at first, but he honestly couldn't believe how much he utterly loved his job now. It was so much better than working with Maura in MI5 and now he actually got to do whatever it took to keep the UK safe. Regardless of what the stupid politicians didn't want him to do.

Maura walked past him and went towards the large TV screen and the fact that they were the two only here for now told Jamie everything he needed to know. Maura was clearly the one who had found the Code Black information and had summoned him and the others here.

Jamie had worked with Maura for over a decade and it wasn't exactly ever a great experience when Maura picked the missions. It was like she always had a sadistic streak where she wanted her agents to suffer and do the most dangerous missions in the Queen's name.

Jamie flat out loved them all so he was just getting more and more excited about finding out what this one was all about.

"You can come in deary," Maura said, picking up a black tablet and connecting it to the TV.

Jamie nodded and went deeper into the headquarters. There was still the subtle hint of ginger beer, sweet cakes and stale beer from the little celebratory drink they had all had last month than had ended up with Jamie knocking over his ginger beer and it had ended up staining the carpet.

Everyone else wasn't too impressed but Jamie had to admit the smell of ginger beer was definitely great.

Jamie went over to Maura who was still in her white blouse, black trousers and black high heels. And even now she still looked amazing compared to Jamie, who had changed out of his "gardening clothes" and into some jeans, checked shirt and trainers. Just so he would look like a normal Londoner and not like a posh high-powered worker like Maura seemed to love looking like.

Maura clicked her fingers and the TV presumably connected to the tablet and Jamie was surprised to see she was bringing up newspaper reports of recent events. There was nothing interesting or major in the reports so he had no clue why she was showing him them.

"Don't worry. Just testing if the connection's working deary," Maura said.

Jamie just smiled. It was just typical of her to tease him.

"Afternoon all," someone said as they stomped through the door.

Jamie looked like and smiled as a very solidly built elderly man wandered over to them wearing a very expensive Italian suit, freshly polished shoes and a head bald enough to become a reflective light in its own right.

It was absolutely brilliant to see Director Harry

Harris alive and well after having to travel to Russia for a top secret mission last week. He might have been pushing seventy but he was so deadly Jamie doubted even Russia's toughest assassins could kill him.

"Good Afternoon Sir," Jamie said, lowering his head enough.

"Enough with that Sir rubbish Jamie. This is Division, not snobbish MI5 or 6," Harry said with a smile.

Jamie really loved working with Harry.

"What you bring us together for Maura?" Harry asked. "Me and Mrs Harris were about to take a dip in the hot tub together and drink and the night away,"

Jamie didn't even know that was still possible at their age but he admired their determination.

Maura nodded her respect towards Harry. "We're still waiting for the twins to show up,"

Again the door opened, two people (two women) walked through and then the door sealed tightly shut.

Jamie smiled as each of the Hill twins were dressed identically in bright red t-shirts, black trousers and white shoes that made them look like clones. He had no idea which one was Harriet and which one was Elena.

The twins even walked perfectly in unison like they were straight out from some kind of horror film.

Both of them might have been from GCHQ, which Jamie liked to just explain away as the UK's version of the US's NSA and in charge of the UK's cyber security, but each of them were so great, funny and really wonderful people to be around. Something that in Jamie's experience was a rarity when it came to nerdy GCGQ people.

"Now we're all here," Maura said, her normal control failing to hide her excitement. "Shall we begin?"

Everyone nodded and Jamie, along with everyone else, leant against the end of the row of desks as they focused on the massive TV screen.

"I wanted to summon you all here because an old friend at MI5 shared this with me," Maura said showing a confidential government email.

Jamie read it, it seemed harmless enough.

"For weeks," Maura said, "MI5 has had good intelligence reports that members of the UK Government are planning to commit a terror attack against its own people and blaming it in on the Scottish nationalists,"

Jamie just felt his stomach twist into a painful knot and everyone else in Division seemed to have the same reaction. It wasn't surprising in the slightest, everyone knew how peaceful, wonderful and great the Scottish people were and they had democratically voted for another independence referendum, so they could be free from the corruption, influence and evil that was the UK Government.

But Jamie knew it was really just about the Scottish people wanting to choose their own future, create their laws and just be themselves without a controlling unloving parent (also known as the UK Government) looking over them.

And given how serious the Scottish people were about getting their freedom through peaceful and democratic means, the entire unionist community was scared of what independence would mean.

So an attack to kill the idea of peaceful nationalism that wanted freedom wasn't exactly a surprise to any Division member.

"Dare I say it," Jamie said, "I take it MI5 had refused to act the intelligence,"

Maura nodded. "MI5 confirmed this morning they will not investigate this potential terror attack and act against the will of the UK Government. Especially not to save the face of the Scottish people,"

"Because English lives are the only lives that matter," Harry said like he was quoting something from a government meeting.

Chances are he was.

Jamie just folded his arms. This was why he left the crap that was MI5 and government work. He had to stop this attack no matter what. He gestured Maura to continue.

"There were a few pieces of evidence about the attack like government emails, money transfers and the early release of several unionist terrorists from jail. Yet dearies, everything seems to be centred around this woman,"

As Maura presumably tried to pull up the photo

of the woman that their first target, Jamie just wanted to punch someone. It was just outrageous that the UK government was going to such extreme lengths just to kill the idea of democratically elected nationalists, that were as far from the idea of right-wing nationalists you could get, and freedom.

Did democracy mean nothing anymore?

"This woman," Maura said.

Jamie instantly heard Harry gasp in delight as everyone looked at the so-called stunning blond in a tight grey trench coat, model-like face and so-called amazing looks that Jamie guessed made most men fall all over her.

Maura laughed. "Exactly Harry. This is Hellen Armstrong, Government Minister for Scotland, and before you say it yes she was born in the South of England so she has no idea what the Scottish people want or need from the Government,"

Jamie loved how savage Maura could be.

"Mrs Armstrong," Maura said, "seems to be the link between all these pieces of evidence of the attack. She is a strong unionist by trade and has actually called for the assassination of the Scottish Government before. If we choose to take this case then she is our first person to investigate,"

Jamie really loved how everyone turned confused for a moment as if it was such a stupid question that Maura was doubting Division would take the case.

It was clear as day why this was a Code Black case, a country's future, democracy and right to choose was at stake. There wasn't a chance in hell Jamie and the others weren't going to take it.

Jamie looked at the others and they all nodded at him.

Jamie went over to Maura. "We're in. What do you want us to do?"

Maura looked like she was so relieved that his answer and she just smiled.

"Put on a suit Jamie. You have a party to go to," Maura said.

Jamie didn't know what she had in mind but it made him more excited than he had been in a long time.

CHAPTER 4
16th September 2022
London, England

The amazing smells of freshly smoked salmon, sweet creamy cakes and smoked bacon filled the massive ballroom as Luca stepped inside, amazed at the sheer scale of the immense ballroom with bright white walls that rose so high into the ceiling before it domed at the top with a stunning chandelier.

Luca liked the wonderful live band that playfully ever so quietly in the background with calming posh music that was just perfect for couples to slow dance to, but he had no intention of doing that tonight.

Luca felt a very tall elegant woman carefully slip her arm under his and he smiled as Alice in all her stunning blue dress and white high heels (the colours of the Scottish flag) had returned from checking in with the First minister of Scotland of what she wanted them to do tonight. Luca wasn't too sure if he wanted to get too involved in that political aspect of the night, but judging by how hot some of the young men were in their expensive tight tailored suits, he definitely wanted to talk to some of them.

Luca slowly led him and Alice into the ballroom and deeper into enemy territory and every one carefully nodded their respects to each other, and carefully gathered in their groups and shunned the outsiders.

This had to be the most clicky party Luca had ever been to and definitely the most unwelcoming. Clearly everyone knew exactly who Alice was and everyone was subtly giving both of them the cold shoulder.

Luca didn't really know why, but it was probably something to do with how Alice could wipe the floor with any political opponent and she had repeatedly embarrassed the Prime Minister in the Houses of Parliament, so maybe this was some kind of petty payback.

As a very hot waiter came up to them, Luca almost wanted to start talking to the guy but then he realised how much disdain and quite frankly, utter hatred the waiter showed towards Alice and himself as they both took drinks. Clearly there wasn't a single friendly face here, it was basically a case of two nationalists in a room of wolfish unionists.

Luca just wanted to laugh at how petty all these men and women were in their expensive clothes as they sneered at Luca and Alice. But he knew it was bad form and the last thing he wanted to do was embarrass Alice and the Scottish Government.

"Spotted how much everyone hates us yet?" Alice asked, smiling.

Luca subtly nodded. "I knew things were bad, but they seriously hate the Scots because they want freedom,"

Alice pretended to take another sip as she led herself and Luca across the ballroom towards a very long row of tables containing amazing looking food.

"Sometimes I forget you were born here. We Scots don't actually hate the English but they hate us with all their heart,"

Luca couldn't disagree and he was surprised when the live band changed to something with more of a beat as an entire group of posh looking men and women in the finest possible clothes entered the ballroom.

Everyone else who was already here bowed like these new people were royalty.

"Who are they?" Luca asked.

Alice shrugged. "Just more members of the UK Government. Oh that's one, the Health Secretary and for some reason there's fifty friends with him,"

Luca was just glad they were all in a very large ballroom capable of holding a good five hundred people. The last thing he wanted was to be in a ballroom jam-packed with people. Regardless of how hot the men were.

"That's who we want," Alice said as she pretended to laugh at Luca like he had just said a joke.

Luca was really impressed at how natural Alice was so it looked like she was just having a good time, instead of plotting the freedom of her country.

"Who?" Luca asked.

Alice subtly gestured to the little blond woman that was strolling into the ballroom with a massive security detail like she owned the place. Luca supposed she was attractive with her long blond hair, little black dress and high heels, but he was only guessing that because of how many of the hot men looked like they were about to faint at her.

That was a shame. All Luca wanted tonight was to meet a nice hot guy. That clearly wasn't going to happen.

"The First Minister wants us to talk to the blond woman, who's actually the Minister of Scotland even though she doesn't understand a single thing our people want or need from the UK Government, and we need to try to get her to support independence,"

Luca just smiled. "Yeah and by the end of the night I'm suddenly going to be straight,"

Alice jokingly frowned at him.

"Sorry I thought we were both saying impossible things,"

Alice playfully hit him. "Behave. I'll talk to her first and you can… go and talk to some of these right-wing unionists. Maybe they'll like you as a doctor,"

Luca gave her a quick kiss on the cheek and he really didn't care to explain to Alice how much right-wingers hated him as a so-called fake doctor, and how much these people hated the very concept of psychology, mental health and therapy.

Luca was just about to start this awful circuit of talking to these hard-line people who would shout and berate him all night when he spotted someone in the sea of other men and women in expensive clothes.

Wow.

Luca focused on a seriously hot sexy man in a very tight fitting and expensive black suit, white shirt and black trousers as he glided so confidently through the crowd.

Luca absolutely loved how the hot man carried himself with such confidence and his stunningly gorgeous face was so smooth and his strong manly jawline was to die for. But the way his longish black hair was styled parted to the left to make him look like a movie-star even more was what really did Luca's heart in.

He was extremely attracted to this drop-dead hunk of a man.

Luca's heart skipped a few beats, his stomach filled with butterflies and sweat started to drip down his back even though it was perfectly cool in the ballroom.

Luca simply took another sip of his drink and just had to talk to that extremely hot man. He might be a typical right-winger who hated him for being gay and being a psychologist but it wasn't like there was anyone hotter to talk to.

And Luca had the sneaky feeling that this man was different. And different was always good.

CHAPTER 5
16th September 2022
London, England

Jamie was really pleased and rather amazed that Maura had a wonderfully expensive suit he could borrow at such short notice, chances were she had probably picked it before she retrieved him earlier today, but he didn't care.

Jamie had been to some amazing high-end parties before but this one certainly didn't top the list by any stretch. Normally government parties were in posh luxurious locations but this ballroom was okay. The chandelier was clearly fake and bright white domed walls made it feel a little small and it was just tacky at the end of the day.

Even the smells of the smoky salmon, bacon and creamy cakes was just pumped into the room, not that anyone at the party knew that. The advantages of working in MI5 and security for so long.

Thankfully the wonderful Hill Twins had already hacked into the security systems and added his name to the guest list, so security was more than willing to let him in when he arrived. And given how his target had arrived at the same time, security was more focused on her anyway.

Jamie wasn't impressed with all the women in their black, golden or red dresses that was supposed to make them look attractive for their husbands, but Jamie had no clue if that was true. The hot men regardless of their age were a little more promising but Jamie just couldn't get over the types of people they were.

Everyone here was either a government minister, donator to the government's political party or just a corrupt business person who gave the government enough money to look the other way. The glory of UK politics never failed to amaze Jamie.

That was another reason why he loved Division. There was no political inference whatsoever.

"Lover boy stop looking at the men," Maura said in his ear.

Jamie hadn't realised the black suit he was wearing was fitted with a hidden camera that send footage back to Division HQ, but that was just wonderfully typical of Maura. Yet Jamie had made sure to double check the invisible earpiece in his left ear before he left. He wanted his team to support him no matter what happened.

"We send you in because unlike Harry here you wouldn't be distracted," Maura said.

Jamie wanted to remind her that he was invisible on missions as proved by the three waiters who had walked towards him and then offered everyone else a drink instead of him, but now wasn't the time.

"Have you got the phone cloner?" the Hill Twins said as one.

Jamie subtly nodded knowing that Division was most certainly in the security cameras of the ballroom to.

Jamie slowly started gliding his way through the crowd of men, women and waiters as they spoke about pointless topics that would only help themselves and not the people they were elected to serve.

"Helen Armstrong is over by the food table. She's talking to someone who works…" Maura said.

Jamie almost reacted to the silence but he forced himself not to.

He kept gliding invisibly through the crowd like nothing was wrong whilst he listened to the loud typing of keyboards through the earpiece.

"Right okay," Maura said carefully. "Helen Armstrong is currently talking to David Fletcher, terrorist convicted two years ago after bombing a building belonging to the Scottish Government and leader of a Far-right Unionist group,"

Jamie rolled his eyes. This wasn't good. He must have been one of the people Helen had released early from prison. If they were talking so openly then Helen must have been confident in whatever she was doing.

"We need that phone cloned now," Maura said.

Jamie subtly nodded and when to glide over there a bit quicker when he knocked into someone.

Jamie was hardly impressed with the idiot that dared tried to stop him. Jamie looked at the man and... fucking hell.

Out of the entire sea of people around them Jamie was so glad to knock into this beautiful young man that was about the same age as him, had the most beautiful sapphire eyes imaginable and such a handsome innocent face.

Jamie thought he had been poisoned or something as he came over all hot, sweaty and like his mouth didn't work anymore. But that was all because of this insanely hot man in front of him.

It took Jamie a few moments longer to realise that both him and the insanely hot man still had their arms touching each other's shoulders from when they had knocked into each other, and Jamie had to admit his training kicked in.

The insanely hot man had a great body with basically no muscle, no weapon or anything except a smartphone in his top pocket. But he still loved the amazing power that flowed between them as Jamie gently rubbed the man's shoulders.

The insanely hot man seemed to enjoy it then they both must have realised who the people around them were and they let go of each other. Jamie hated letting go of the hottie and he really wanted to keep touching him, exchanging glances and just getting to know him better but he did have a mission.

"Um, sorry to knock you," the Hottie said.

Jamie forced his mouth to work but the Hottie was just too beautiful and stunning for his brain and mouth to work.

"For god sake," Maura said, clearly having finishing laughing over something. "Use your mouth, don't kiss him before you think of it, and talk,"

Jamie nodded. "It's fine. It was my fault,"

"Finish this up," Maura said. "Target is on the move. Seems to be leaving,"

Jamie wanted to rush off but he really wanted to focus on this beautiful man a little more. But he did have a job to do.

"Um," Jamie said. "I have to go. What's your name? Can I call you?"

The Hottie laughed at how flustered he was getting, Jamie felt like such a schoolboy.

"Dr Luca Kelly," the Hottie said.

That was a hot name that Jamie was definitely going to be repeating so he didn't forget it.

"Target is leaving!" Maura shouted.

"I'll call you," Jamie said.

"You don't have my number," Luca said.

Jamie smiled and shrugged. "I'll find you. It's what I do,"

Jamie quickly glided through the crowd and saw Helen in all her blondness almost at the exit that was nothing more than a green fire escape.

Jamie waved at her and she stopped. The four security guards near her tensed.

"Minister," Jamie said, gesturing to come closer. "MI5 Officer Jamie Owl, can I have a word,"

"Your fake last name was original," Maura said.

Helen smiled and came over to Jamie. "Yes what can I do for you Officer?"

Jamie moved a little closer to her in hopes of getting the Phone Cloner in range.

"Cloning is starting," the Hill Twins said as one.

"Minister, we at MI5 have had some reports of people sending you hate and death threats. I'm leading a new taskforce at MI5 aiming to crack down on harassment against Members of Parliament like yourself,"

Jamie was rather impressed with that lie actually.

"Of course," Helen said, moving even closer. "Personally I think those left-wing idiots who put you up to this are pathetic. The UK Government knows hate and death threats are part of life, and because we aren't sissies we don't need MI5 wasting resources on this pet project,"

"20% done," Maura said.

"I completely agree Minister," Jamie said. "But I am just trying to do my job so are there any people in particular you're concerned about?"

"25%," Maura said. "Keep her talking,"

Helen leant forward and nodded. "It's the Scots you need. The UK Government keeps trying to deliver them our vision for a new more enlightened and less barbaric Scotland but they are so resistant to change. I would like to see them become more civilised but they are threatening me,"

Jamie forced himself not to laugh as Maura, Harry and the Hill Twins were laughing in his ear. Helen was completely delusional, considering Scotland was leading the UK in terms of Higher Education and all the pillars of modern society.

"Of course Minister. I will look into it," Jamie said.

Helen turned to leave.

"We need more time. We don't have phone records yet," Maura asked.

Jamie went to go over to her but the security guards stopped him and Jamie didn't feel like making a scene here.

Not so close to beautiful stunning Luca.

"Damn it," Maura said. "We only have 32% of her phone cloned. Well done anyway. Finish up and regroup here,"

Jamie nodded as Maura cut the link and even though he completely knew that Maura wasn't mad at him.

Jamie was mad at himself.

Something big was going down and he just felt like he had blown it.

All because of some insanely hot man that he didn't even know.

CHAPTER 6
17th September 2022
London, England

Even though the entire night was an absolute burst for converting unionists to supporting them, getting any sort of respect and getting any hot guys to be interested in him, Luca still absolutely loved tonight.

Luca sat in the very comfortable backseat of a black SUV as their driver (that Alice paid for personally because like the majority of the Scottish Government she hated using taxpayer money for something as trivial as her own security) gently drove them back to his and Alice's separate apartments.

Luca always loved the wonderful fresh car smell of the SUV that made it smell of new and refreshing.

As Alice finished up a phone call with the First Minister about the progress of the party, Luca didn't really care to listen too much because he just couldn't stop thinking about that hot sexy man who he had knocked into.

Luca hadn't even meant to knock into him, he just wanted to talk to the amazing looking guy, but he had seen in such a hurry. Normally would take that as a sad sign that the guy was being nice wasn't interested in him in the slightest. And chances are as he was at that party, he wasn't even gay.

But it was how speechless, sexy and smiley the hot man seemed that made Luca get hopeful. Even now he was only thinking about him and Luca felt his hands turn clammy and his stomach filled with butterflies and his wayward parts got excited.

Luca watched as the SUV drove past the stunning River Thames that shone a wide range of beautiful lights illuminating bright skyscrapers that rose up like claws into the sky through the darkness.

"Of course First Minister. I will keep you informed. Tell Chris I said *Hi* and have a good evening," Alice said as she hung up.

Luca wanted to ask how the call went but Alice huffed a little and just rested her head against the window. It was flat out impossible that the First Minister of Scotland had moaned at Alice because this was expected and the call was more of a social one than anything serious. But clearly Alice was still upset by the lack of progress.

Luca almost felt the same way but he was too focused on the sexy man. And it was just strange how he said he would find Luca. Like who the hell was he if he could track down Luca by himself?

There was something both very hot about that but also a tat weird. Yet the last feeling this sexy man gave him was a dangerous vibe.

Oddly enough Luca just wanted to see him again and get to knock him better.

"Thinking about your man from the party?" Alice asked, not looking away from the car window.

Luca moved uncomfortably in his seat. He didn't know what to say or do or if his best friend would be concerned or angry at him.

He almost wanted to just look out the window as the SUV turned a street corner and started to go down a very dark narrow road that was probably meant to be a shortcut but looked like the start of something more evil.

"He looked nice," Alice said. "But please be careful,"

Luca looked at her. "Why?"

"Beaut," Alice said looking at him. "We were in a room of right-wingers who work for the UK Government. The same UK Government that had refused to act on any LGBT+ equality recommendations from their own Equality Advisors before they all resigned because of the lack of interest from the government,"

"I know," Luca said.

Alice gently placed her hand on his. "I just don't want you getting hurt by any of them. And they saw us walk in together, they know you're connected to the Scottish Government somehow. I wouldn't be surprised if whose homophobes are already planning which one will *bed a sissy for Queen and Country*,"

Luca wanted to say the people at the party wouldn't do that, but he had already seen plenty of government ministers and official make homophobic comments on live TV, and of course nothing bad ever happened to them.

Alice gently kissed Luca on the cheek. "I just want you to be okay,"

Luca smiled. He could look after himself that was a fact but it was great to know that he had a powerful ally by his side.

"How did the call with the First Minister go?" Luca asked.

Thankfully the SUV came out onto a very bright and busy main road with tall hotels lining it, and tons of cars and vans driving around them.

"She's great. She's glad we had fun but I told her about something I saw," Alice said.

"What?" Luca asked.

"What do you know of the Edinburgh Bombings two years ago?" Alice asked.

"I was in Inverness at the time. I remember there were two bombings in 24 hours done by three men against buildings of Scottish Politicians all nationalists," Luca said.

Alice seemed impressed. "I saw one of them tonight. And the First Minister checked with one of her few friends left at the UK's Ministry of Justice and all three of them were strangely released early,"

Luca just cocked his head. That was outrageous. Why the hell would three known terrorists be allowed out? And most importantly on what grounds would they be allowed out on?

Alice carefully looked behind and around the SUV as it kept driving, Luca was sure they weren't being followed but he wasn't great at spotting that sort of thing. He didn't need to before now.

Then Alice leant in closer almost as if she didn't trust the driver completely.

"I think," Alice said, "the UK Government is planning something against us. I know it's crazy but the First Minister still has some loyal friends in MI5, 6 and counterterrorism. Everyone has received chatter later of an attack but no agency is acting on it,"

Luca felt his throat dry up. He didn't want to be hearing this, it was flat out illegal, but clearly that didn't matter to the UK Government. Anyone just needed to turn on the TV these days, but this was something on a much grander scale.

Alice went so close to Luca's ear, that he felt her warm breath on his.

"I don't want to bring in my Members of Parliament that sit with me in the UK Parliament into this, but I would like you on my side. Can you help me try to figure this out?" Alice asked.

Luca was about to say no. He wasn't a spy or anything, but he had never ever heard Alice so scared, concerned and frightened in all the years he had known her. Even when she was in his therapy room she never sounded this scared like so many other first-timers were.

Alice was truly scared.

Luca nodded. "What must I do?"

"Driver," Alice said. "Take Dr Kelly to my apartment please,"

Luca just smiled. Clearly she was planning something and he just hoped that she was wrong about all this.

Because if she wasn't then he couldn't even imagine the consequences for the entire United Kingdom.

And Luca really, really wanted to talk to that amazing sexy man from the party again. He didn't know why.

He only knew that he did.

CHAPTER 7
17th September 2022
London, England

"Background check is completely negative,"

When Jamie stepped back into Division Headquarters with its jet black walls, massive TV screens and rows of computers on desks. The last thing he expected to see was Harry, Maura and the Hill Twins just standing in front of the TV with their hands behind their backs.

He had been working with Division long enough to know that his friends were definitely crazy at times. But this was certainly a new type of crazy for them all.

Jamie had been expecting them all to be hunched over computers or staring at the TV as all of them tried to search for the secret or key that would unlock what the hell was going on here.

But none of that was clearly happening.

Jamie went over to them all and clearly they had had Chinese foods judging by the overflowing metal rubbish bin under the desks. And judging by the smell someone had orange chicken, shrimp curry and something with duck in it. It all smelt amazing but it didn't explain what was going on.

"I'm sorry I screwed up," Jamie said.

Maura and Harry laughed like he was being silly.

"Granted," Harry asked, who now looked like a really old man and with his professor-like glasses on. "We would have preferred Helen not to know you were MI5 and wanted to talk to you. But Division is flexible,"

Jamie just smiled as he really wanted to be flexible in bed with that insanely hot Luca Kelly. Ever since Jamie left the party he hadn't thought or dared to think about anything else.

His name alone *Luca* was so hot and beautiful on the tongue. Jamie seriously wanted to know who he was, what he liked and he just wanted to go out on a date with that stunning man.

Then it clicked. Jamie knew exactly why all his friends were standing in front of the TV screen.

"You looked him up, didn't you?" Jamie asked.

Harry slowly nodded and smiled. "We won't tell you everything about him but you getting to know him might be a good idea,"

Jamie didn't have the heart to tell his boss that he would have asked Luca out on a date even if they all forbidden him. He liked beautiful Luca that much.

"Dr Luca Kelly," Maura said, "and no we will not tell you what he is a doctor in, sometimes works for the Scottish Government. He attended tonight with the Scottish Government UK Parliamentary Political Party leader Alice Zelly,"

Jamie wasn't a fan of how much his friends were teasing him. He just wanted to know every little amazing thing about that skinny sexy hunk of a man.

"And there is reason to believe Alice Zelly believes something is up," Maura said.

The Hill Twins each took out a tablet and activated the TV screen showing CCTV footage of Alice watching Helen and the terrorist David Fletcher. She was clearly shocked, but it was impressive how she forced herself not to physically react. But Jamie could tell she wasn't impressed.

"I presume she made a call to the First Minister," Jamie said.

Harry nodded. "Thankfully we were monitoring the calls. Alice called the First Minister as they drove home, the First Minister called some loyal friends who checked it out. Thankfully I made sure the Hill Twins covered the agents' tracks,"

Jamie nodded his thanks to the twins. The last thing Scotland needed right now was their only few friends within the intelligence services being "resigned" (sacked).

"That isn't our concern for the moment," Jamie said.

He wanted to add that he was more concerned about the beautiful Luca and how badly he wanted to go out with him, but he was relieved when Maura bought up Helen's phone records.

"We managed to get some good information from the phone," Maura said.

"Yeah," the Hill Twins said as one. "The woman has clearly never heard of the word *delete*. It will take us at least two days to go through the information. We're actually grateful you didn't download the entire phone,"

Jamie knew that the twins weren't being mean but he was still annoyed at himself.

"And with the twins focusing on the phone data," Harry said, really looking like an old professor as he slid the glasses down his nose. "I will invite my MI6 friends to dinner tomorrow night for some covert talking,"

Jamie wanted to say don't to Harry because if the intelligence services were avoiding this attack on purpose then it was dangerous revealing Division knew about it. But if anyone could handle themselves, it would certainly be Harry.

"Meanwhile dearies." Maura said, "I will be following Helen to see if she meets up with any more conspirators this weekend. Let's hope she doesn't, but I have a feeling she will. Especially now she knows MI5 was talking to her,"

Before Harry and Maura left they both hugged him and that was really how Jamie knew they weren't mad with him. But he was normally so professional and focused, yet that stunning Luca had made him fall apart and lose his professionalism.

Jamie was about to leave himself when the two Hill Twins smiled at him and each held out a post-it note. Jamie took them both and he just smiled.

Each one had the address of either Alice or Luca. He was definitely going to pay Luca a visit in a few hours' time and he was really hoping he was going to be in.

And most importantly actually wanted to see him.

Jamie was so excited for the visit he raced home to make sure he looked his best for such a stunning man.

CHAPTER 8
17th September 2022
London, England

Luca couldn't believe how great last night had been, especially when him and Alice had gone back to her stunningly elegant, spacious and extremely modern London apartment (that again Alice had to have paid for personally to avoid *wasting* taxpayer money). Luca was almost sad to leave this morning.

But as he stepped out of the elevator of Alice's apartment building into the very bright white marble covered lobby, he was more than impressed. Last night had been such a blur when they had returned to some plotting that he hadn't had time to focus on the lobby. But it was simply stunning with its constant rich aroma of fresh mint and freshly cut grass (how they got the aroma into the lobby he didn't know) and because the lobby only had a great-looking white marble desk in the centre, a row of chairs to Luca's left and free lemon-flavoured water on a golden table to his right. Luca was very glad to have a friend staying in such an amazing place.

"Hi there," a man with a very sexy voice said.

Luca looked around for a moment and noticed there was a rather attractive man standing next to the lemon-flavoured water table. He looked great with his broad shoulders, great muscles and he looked like a movie star.

Then Luca twigged that the hot man might have been out of his tight black suit, amazingly white shirt and black shoes. But he still looked simply stunning into his sexy black tight jeans, red checked shirt and hiking boots.

"Hi," Luca said, amazed his mouth actually worked. "So you found me,"

Clearly that made the hot man look a little awkward but Luca still went straight over to him. He smelt so wonderful with his earthy, piney aftershave.

"Walk with me," Luca said, gesturing to the bright white marble exit with gold veining running through it on the far side of the lobby.

"Sure," the hot man said, smiling like a schoolboy.

That was cute.

"How did you find me?" Luca asked.

The hot man almost laughed. "Shouldn't I give you my name first? And I'm a cop from the London Metropolitan Police. Me and a group of others were drafted into providing security for the event,"

Luca almost felt silly for not even asking the hot

man's name, but his brief explanation about his job sounded great and it actually explained why he had managed to find Luca.

As part of the security for the event, everyone had to add their address in the registration details so Luca really doubted it would be that difficult to find his or Alice's address in their records.

Luca felt his stomach twist into a painful knot at that realisation. Him and Alice hadn't exactly done too much plotting last night because Alice had been rather tired actually (probably more from the stress of a potential attack against them more than the party itself) but if they did get involved in spying on the unionists. Then surely it wouldn't be hard for their enemies to find Alice's address too.

He had to warn her about that later on.

Luca almost jumped as the hot man gently touched his shoulder as they passed the check-in desk in the centre of the lobby.

"Everything okay?" the hot man asked. "I'm Charles. Do you not like cops?"

Luca quickly looked at him to see if he was offended. But he wasn't. Instead Charles simply had such an amazing smile and Luca seriously loved the feeling of him touching his shoulder.

"No sorry. It's just work stuff. My father was actually a cop in Kent Police before he... died,"

Charles walked quickly ahead of Luca almost as if he was trying to catch the large glass doors that Luca hadn't really focused on too much either until now.

Luca watched some of the other guests who were hidden in the corners of the lobby look strangely at Charles like he was mad for trying to open the doors himself. That was when Luca clocked there were two hotel staff members standing outside who presumably opened the doors for them.

"I'm sorry to hear that. I wasn't trying to pride," Charles said.

Luca loved how caringly he said that, maybe he was actually a wonderful man. Normally when men said that there was always a hint of apathy to it as they were always trying to get into his trousers.

But Charles was different.

"It's okay, and you know at this hotel they open the doors for you?" Luca said.

Luca loved how embarrassed Charles looked, like he actually knew that but he had forgotten it for some reason.

The large glass doors opened for them and Luca and Charles both went out onto the surprisingly empty London pavement with not a single other person nor car walking on the path or the very wide road. Luca liked how very tall skyscrapers (that were other apartment blocks) lined the road, and he really wanted to find out more about this cop that had tracked him down.

"You know," Luca said, "I suppose you want to ask me something if you bothered to track me down like a stalker,"

It was so cute how Charles looked to the ground

like a shy schoolboy, and it took everything Luca had not to go forward and hug him, and hopefully kiss him.

"Yeah actually," Charles said. "There's this cool vegan coffee shop round the corner if you had time for a chat,"

Luca bit his lip. It was so cute seeing Charles nervous and almost scared of getting a rejection, but the vegan comment was strange. It was something that Luca rarely mentioned to people.

"Did you get my dieting info from the party too?" Luca asked.

Charles looked into his eyes, and Luca felt his hands turn very clammy at that moment.

"No," Charles said. "I just prefer vegan drinks and food. I had no idea you liked it too,"

Luca smiled and put out his arm to Charles. Maybe if he liked vegan stuff there were other amazing things they had in common.

And Luca just couldn't wait to find out even more about this hot handsome stranger who had bothered to track him down.

CHAPTER 9
16th September 2022
London, England

What the hell had Jamie done.

All Jamie had wanted to do was just go and see that outrageously hot sexy man from last night and maybe ask him out. He had absolutely not meant to tell hottie Luca he was a cop and given him a fake name. That was not cool in the slightest, but it was just so natural for him to lie.

But he didn't want to lie to this insanely hot man.

Jamie pretended (really pretended) to be all calm as he sat down on a very cold wooden chair at a little oak table at the very back of *Sarah's Vegan Treats*. It was a great restaurant with rows upon rows of little round tables, and even this early in the morning (10 am) the place was packed and filled with the constant sound of people talking and laughing and debating the latest social media trend like all good Londoners did.

Jamie looked at Luca studying the little card menu with his stunning sapphire eyes bright and wide like he was a kid in a candy store. He was so damn beautiful and Jamie felt like the luckiest man in the world to at the privilege of spending time with this hottie.

"So how was the security at the party last night?" Luca asked, running his finger down the menu.

"Very good. There weren't any incidents, why do you ask?" Jamie asked.

Luca checked if there was anything on the back of the menu (there wasn't Jamie had been here too many times to know that) and Luca simply stared into Jamie's eyes. Jamie flat out loved looking into Luca's beautiful sapphires.

"You know who my boss and friend is?" Luca asked.

Jamie shrugged. It was technically a little lie but he actually didn't know that much about this cutie. Maura hadn't exactly wanted to tell him too much.

"Alice Zelly, leader of the Scottish Government's Party in Westminster," Luca said with such conviction and pride.

There was something strangely refreshing about seeing someone else who loved their political connections as much as him. Granted Jamie rarely spoke about his own beliefs, but it was really cute seeing Luca get excited.

Then Luca's face sort of turned into a bit of confusion.

"Something wrong?" Jamie asked, concerned he had done something wrong.

Luca laughed and waved over a waitress that was walking past. Jamie ordered himself a very large vegan chai latte, and Luca ordered himself a normal-large vegan hot chocolate.

Jamie felt like his heart melted. There was just something so sweet about men ordering hot chocolate on a first date.

"Sorry," Luca said. "It's just in my experience most English are either extremely hateful or passionate when I mention who my best friend is. Vast majority of them fall into the former category,"

Jamie just shook his head. Even if he didn't support Scottish Independence, he would still at least have the decency to respect the people that did, just like how he had some respect towards the unionists. Even though he didn't understand their arguments, but that was just testament to the way the UK was marching.

People either believed in what the ruling government believed in, or were seen as a crazy.

"I like her opinions and I think the Scots are great," Jamie said. "But what do you do for them? I mean like as a job. You know I'm a cop,"

Jamie hated lying but he was committed now.

Jamie loved how Luca's face lit up.

"I actually don't work for the Scottish Government in any official capacity. I'm a psychologist during the week,"

Jamie smiled. "Brilliant, what do you specialise in? Treating mental health, treating mental processes or teaching?"

Jamie was a little confused when Luca's mouth dropped and his eyes lit up as he stared at Jamie.

"Wow," Luca said. "Most people ask me some rubbish about profiling that isn't psychology, or just roll their eyes and ask me why am I wasting my life,"

Jamie laughed. His first boyfriend had studied psychology at university and told him about all the struggles he faced at home and from others about the choice of his degree.

"Those people who don't realise psychology's important are just silly," Jamie said, harshly.

"Here you go boys," the waitress said as she gave Jamie his latte and Luca his hot chocolate.

"Thank you," they both said.

Jamie took a mouthful of the latte and it was the most delicious creamiest latte he had ever had. The rich bitterness of the coffee, the velvety smoothness of the vegan milk and the sugary decadence of the vanilla all combined to create a sensational symphony of flavour in his mouth.

Jamie really loved this restaurant.

"I wish my mum and sister would understand that," Luca said.

Jamie found it a little sad that Luca's family didn't support him in the slightest, but that was just life to Jamie as well. He still hated how his parents had kicked him out for being gay calling him an unholy abomination and the rest.

"Yeah," Jamie said. "Sometimes family sucks,"

Jamie almost fainted as Luca took his hand and gently rubbed it. Jamie was amazed to see there was such a great twinkle to Luca's sapphire eyes that seemed to create a little bit of magic between them.

Jamie would have loved to spend the entire day, and ideally weekend, with this insanely hot man. But Jamie knew that at some point he needed to check in with Division.

If him and Luca ever did develop a relationship and the UK Government did launch an attack that blamed the Scots then their love could never ever happen.

And that terrified Jamie.

CHAPTER 10
19th September 2022
London, England

After an absolutely wonderful weekend with that sexy hunk of a man Charles where they had gone out for dinner, lunch and had some romantic walks through some of London's parks (which Luca had no idea there were so many), Luca couldn't believe how happy, positive and as light as a feather he felt. Charles just made him feel so alive, cared for and just brilliant.

The best Luca had felt in a long time.

On the Monday morning, Luca stepped out of the very busy elevator as the sea of his fellow psychologists in all their different heights, sizes and classes rushed out to get to their desks, and Luca stepped out into the main area of their floor where there were rows upon rows of little white office-like cubicles.

Luca was more than glad to have his own

personal office that was so bright and private. He would have hated to have to share therapy rooms like the psychologists out here did. He wasn't a fan of everything in the main area from the tiny cubicles to the glaring fake lights on the ceiling to the constant hum of ventilation systems overhead that fed the rest of the building.

It wasn't his idea of a fun workday.

"Dr Kelly?" a woman asked.

Luca looked towards his office and forced himself not to frown when he saw a very uncomfortable Alice wearing a rather attractive black dress with two women in black suits and dark sunglasses behind her. And Luca didn't need to be a hot Met cop to know that these two women had guns under their suits.

Luca subtly looked at Alice in case she gave him a sign to just run or something, but she gave him a half-hearted kind smile like she was a protective mother trying to comfort her scared child.

Alice definitely wasn't his mother but she was a damn fine best friend. If she wasn't telling him to run then he was going to trust her.

Luca simply went through the main area, smiled at other psychologists and let the three women carefully walk behind him. He wasn't going to be scared in his own workplace. This was his domain after all.

Luca went up to the bright white wooden door of his office and looked at the two women in dark suits.

"We may speak in here if that is convenient for Her Majesty's Government," Luca said.

The two women looked surprised they had been spotted that easily, but Luca didn't get why. There weren't that many security agencies in the UK and they weren't exactly known for being creative with their dress sense.

Luca popped open the door and went straight over to his bright modern desk and he gestured the women to look around his very modern, spacious and wonderfully bright office. He wasn't sure why he did it but he just wanted them to know he had a good job.

"They picked me up on the way to work too," Alice said.

"We needed to warn you both," the tallest of the two women said.

"About what?" Luca asked, harshly.

The shorter woman took out her phone and showed him and Alice photos of Alice failing to follow Helen Armstrong subtly.

"We know you nationalists are up to something. Everyone in MI5 and Counter-Terrorism knows. As members of the UK Government, you are-"

"We are NOT members of the UK Government," Luca said.

He had no clue where that anger came from but he was flat out not being tainted with their corrupt brush and he was a proud Scot that just wanted his country to be free. Not a mere political football to the overweight and corrupt politicians in Westminster.

Alice pretended to clap until one of the women shot her a warning look.

"We have tapped your phones," the taller woman said. "We know you are conspiring with the First Minister of Scotland. We know she is a terrorist and plotting to destroy the United Kingdom,"

Luca just laughed at the stupidity of these agents. Since when was peacefully and democratically wanting freedom anyway related to terrorism?

The two women in dark suits simply shook their heads in frustration.

"As you two will not listen," the shorter woman said, "I will warn you plain and simple. In the next few weeks we would have gathered enough information and evidence to charge you both, the First Minister and every single Scottish Nationalist with terrorism charges. I highly suggest you quiet your roles in the Scottish Government to save yourself,"

Luca and Alice just stood in cold silence as the two women left Luca's office and Luca felt his blood boil. Then he looked around his office, even more so where the two women had been, just in case they left listening devices.

Alice passed Luca a little USB stick that looked small enough to fit into his phone. Alice plugged it in and so did Luca.

"That should be okay for now," Alice said. "The First Minister got this from a friend in the Secret

Service, our phones can't be tapped or hacked for now,"

That was little relief.

"What did you learn?" Luca asked.

Alice shrugged. "Not a lot. Helen was meeting with a lot of Government officials. I saw David Fletcher, the terrorist, out in public with her and two other released terrorists that had joined him in the bombings two years ago,"

Luca seriously didn't like what he was hearing. This was far from good news and at the end of the day they were just amateur spies or people trying to stop this and it wasn't like they could trust an actual spy with this matter.

They were alone.

Luca's eyes narrowed as Alice came over to him and wrapped her arms round him. "I think we need to stop talking for a while. Let me deal with this,"

"Like fuck am I," Luca said. "Scotland is my country too and you're my best friend. I am not having the UK Government create some *evidence* to imprison you and my other friends. We are doing nothing wrong,"

Alice gave him a weak smile. "Who's that guy you were on a few dates with over the weekend?"

Luca's face lit up. It had been such a brilliant weekend that he never wanted it to end but he didn't like where Alice was going.

"He's a Met cop. He likes you and supports us but... I don't think we should bring him into this.

And what can he do? He works for the Met police, not an intelligence agency," Luca said.

Alice nodded and threw her hands up in the air.

"I'll call you later after work," Alice said. "Hopefully, me, the First Minister and others can figure out our next move. And as the English say *good day,*"

Luca shook his head and smiled. "Good day to you too my dear,"

Luca watched his office door shut behind her and his stomach filled with both butterflies and twisted into a painful knot.

It definitely felt like the walls were closing in on Luca's freedom but he couldn't deny he really wanted to spend more time and work next to that hot sexy Charles.

That would almost be a treat in itself.

CHAPTER 11
19th September 2022
London, England

"Well this is a bit of a clusterfuck,"

As Jamie sat on a very comfortable wooden chair with the jet black walls and rows of desks and computers behind him in Division Headquarters, that was the very last thing he had been expecting the Hill Twins to say as one.

Maura still wasn't in yet and neither was Harry which was beyond strange as both of them normally got into the office at about six o'clock in the morning. It was now ten.

Jamie was a tat concerned about them both but considering how everyone (maybe minus the Hill Twins) were highly trained Government assassins, he knew that they could and definitely would handle themselves.

A few moments later the thick smell of bitter coffee, sweet caramel and freshly baked Danish pastries that would melt in Jamie's mouth in buttery deliciousness filled the air as Maura and Harry, holding coffee for everyone, finally came in.

"Don't even ask," Maura said, carrying a brown bag of Danish for everyone.

Jamie was more concerned about what everyone was wearing. The Hill Twins were still wearing the same red jumper and other clothes from two days ago, Maura was wearing a white blouse and white jeans (she never normally got that colour coordinated) and Harry seriously looked like an old man.

Jamie was rather pleased he was in his checked shirt and jeans.

"Stupid Met cops have closed a main road so it was a nightmare to get here folks," Harry said.

Jamie nodded his thanks to Harry as he passed him a very large vegan cappuccino.

"How did everyone's mission get on then?" Jamie asked.

Everyone nodded at the Hill Twins as they stood there in front of the large TV grinning. Then Jamie remembered the Clusterfuck comment.

"We couldn't recover a lot of the texts, photos and files on the phone as we had less than half of it," one of the Twins said (probably Harriet going on past experience).

"But we managed to retrieve several emails about purchases made on Government accounts and paid for with taxpayer money," the other one said (probably Elena).

"That explains what I saw," Maura said. "I saw Helen meeting in board daylight three known terrorists that were released recently and several corrupt Government Ministers,"

Jamie wanted to point out that basically everyone in the Government was corrupt at this point but that seemed unneeded.

"The purchases were for," Harriet said, "large amounts of C4, blasting caps and a lot of fireworks,"

Jamie wasn't surprised Helen had paid for it with Government money, it was easier to explain it away like that. The rules made it impossible to do that, but the rules were more like guidelines at this point. So if someone found out Helen could easily say the Ministry of Defence asked her to buy it using funds her department didn't need.

It was stupid but clearly an effective lie.

Jamie shook his head to Maura as she offered him a very crispy and amazing looking Danish.

"What about your date mission?" Maura asked.

Jamie felt sweat form on his forehead, his hands turned clammy and his wayward parts flared to life. It had just been such an amazing, almost magical weekend with Luca.

"Very good thank you," Jamie said. "He thinks I'm a Met cop and my name is Charles,"

"Charles?" Harry said. "That is a very pompous and silly name,"

Jamie leant forward. "And what is your real name, *Harry?*"

"Horatio," Harry said quietly.

Everyone laughed quietly.

"Did you manage to get anything out of him?" Maura asked.

Jamie looked at the floor. He knew he was probably meant to get some information out of the hottie, but he had just been so caught up in all their happy, wonderfully magical moments together that he hadn't.

"As an intelligence officer I was working the asset to establish a rapport with the subject," Jamie said coldly. "Then in future interactions I would press the asset to reveal information,"

Everyone gave him a mocking smile.

"I will. Promise," Jamie said.

"Good," the Hill Twins said as one. "Because that was another reason why this was a clusterfuck. We hacked into Luca's office and noticed two MI5 agents were there,"

Jamie took a deep breath of the coffee-scented air. This wasn't good.

"Then we hacked into Luca's phone before he added some kind of crazy good security to it," Harriet said. "And the agents said the Government is preparing evidence to arrest all the nationalists, including Luca and Alice,"

Jamie threw his arms up in the air. That was absolutely ridiculous. All these people wanted was a bit of freedom and these stupid unionists were planning something. Jamie had to protect Luca no matter the cost, everyone in Division had to solve it.

"Harry," Jamie said. "Please tell me you have something, anything from your meeting with your MI6 friends,"

Harry huffed and took a massive sip of his coffee.

"Nothing. All my friends rejected my offer, sent warning after warning about Division needing to stay out of it and then I get a rock thrown through my window last night,"

Jamie just shook his head. This was so pathetic but at least Division knew that they were scaring the Government and everyone else involved in the conspiracy.

But as the Hill Twins bought up Luca's and Alice's pictures onto the TV screen. Jamie couldn't help but stare at the extremely cute man on the screen, he just had to protect him regardless of the consequences.

Jamie had let cute hot men down before as an Intelligence Officer. He wasn't going to let Luca down.

Even though their relationship was completely built on a lie.

CHAPTER 12
21ˢᵗ September 2022
London, England

Even the delightful hints of apples, pineapples and limes that filled the crispy refreshing air wasn't enough to relax Luca as he stood against the cold brick of a London restaurant with tons of Londoners drinking and smoking around him. This wasn't the normal sort of place where Luca wanted to meet people, especially really cute men, but he wasn't exactly sure of himself at the moment.

Luca focused on the busy wide main road in front of him with an endless stream of black taxis, red London buses and more normal smaller tourist cars driving up and down the road.

He had been waiting for two days for Alice to call him about what their next moves were, she hadn't called him. Luca had tried to call, text and see if she was at her office. She wasn't.

Luca had even had the privilege of calling the

First Minister of Scotland to see if she knew where Alice was, but she didn't. And that had only alarmed the First Minister more and more, it hadn't dawned on Luca before that phone call how close her and Alice actually were.

"You called," Charles said as he wrapped his wonderfully strong sexy arms around Luca and kissed him on the head.

Luca almost orgasmed at the sheer power and love he felt in the kiss. Luca just collapsed into Charles's amazing body and seriously loved feeling his powerful back muscles as he returned the hug.

Luca wasn't exactly sure why he had called Charles, but given how he was a Met cop and his best friend was missing, and then there were the warnings from MI5. Luca didn't know who else to turn to, and he just felt so safe, secure and protected around stunning Charles.

"Thank you," Luca said resting his chin on Charles's well-muscled shoulders.

Charles pulled away and gestured for them to walk. Luca didn't know how Charles had guessed the call wasn't a date or an offer for dinner, but he was amazed that he had.

Luca smiled and led them along the slightly narrow London pavement where different people stood talking, drinking and laughing with each other after a hard day's work. And Luca had a feeling that there were far too many people here for anyone to try anything.

"You sounded concerned on the phone. What's up?" Charles asked.

"I need to know can you look into something quietly for me," Luca said.

Charles wrapped an arm around Luca's waist and that definitely made him go lightheaded. He loved that feeling of Charles touching him.

"Why?" Charles said thoughtfully.

"I cannot say but I would like an answer please," Luca said.

Luca leant to one side as a mother and two young children walked past, and then he smiled as the two children asked why him and Charles were walking like that.

"The Met can investigate anything if there's evidence of a crime," Charles said.

That was exactly what Luca had been concerned about. He didn't have any evidence that Alice was missing or anything, he only had a feeling.

A bad one at that.

Charles looked behind them, Luca didn't know why, but he didn't focus on it.

"You have to tell me now. What crime might have been committed? Are you okay? Are you hurt?"

Luca kissed Charles on the lips as a thanks for the concern, and then he quickly realised that was their first proper kiss. And it felt utterly amazing.

Charles pulled Luca so close to him that Luca felt his warm breath on his ear. "We can do a lot of that if you tell me you're okay or not,"

Luca definitely wouldn't mind more of that. "I'm not sure but me and Alice were threatened two days ago from people from the UK Government. They were threatening to arrest us and now Alice is missing. I cannot reach her and no one else knows where she is,"

Charles nodded and again looked behind them. That was just getting weird.

"Can you do anything?" Luca asked.

Charles looked unsure. "Not officially, but I can at least check some security footage and ask about, if you want,"

Luca was surprised for some reason. He had been suspecting a complete rejection from Charles telling him that there was no evidence to go on. But maybe this hot sexy man did like him enough to bend a rule or two for him.

Luca really respected him for that.

Then Charles pulled him close and made them walk a little quicker.

"What's wrong?" Luca asked quietly as they cross a side street.

"You have a shadow. You're being followed. Don't look. There's a man dark suit and sunglasses. MI5 probably," Charles said.

Luca felt cold sweat roll down his back. How the hell did Charles know those things?

"What have you and your friend got into" Charles asked as they hurried up a little more.

Luca almost knocked a yoga mum over.

"Nothing. We were just investigating a conspiracy we discovered. Helen Armstrong has been meeting up with terrorists lately,"

Luca wished he could tell this sexy man more but Alice was meant to be investigating. Not him.

Luca heard a loud rumble of a lorry drive up next to them. It indicated it was going to turn into a narrow side street upcoming.

"Hurry. Cross the side street," Charles said.

"Stop! MI5!" someone shouted.

Charles released Luca. Luca ran as fast as he could.

The lorry was starting to turn.

Charles was on the other side of the side street.

Luca ran faster.

He felt someone's fingers brush his back.

Luca legged it.

The lorry turned into the side street.

Luca jumped across the side street. Almost being smashed by the lorry.

Luca felt Charles grab him and drag him away as they both quickly walked away.

"Go to your apartment or where you live," Charles said looking around. "I need to talk to my boss about this. Can I come over later?"

Luca's heart almost stopped at that amazing offer but he focused. This wasn't the time for romance (regardless of how badly he wanted it).

"Sure. I live in-" Luca said.

Charles put a wonderfully soft finger against

Luca's lips. Luca wanted to kiss Charles so badly.

"Don't say it here. You don't know who's about. I'll find the address. Just stay safe. I'll be around later," Charles said.

Charles was about to walk off when Luca grabbed his hand and kissed him. Luca loved the amazing feeling of Charles's soft sensational lips against his.

It was just as out-of-this-world as he imagined.

Charles broke the kiss and just smiled like a schoolboy at him. "I'll see you later and maybe he can do a little more,"

Charles gave him a quick kiss and simply walked away turning invisible into the crowd.

Luca wanted to just stop for a moment and savour the wonderful taste of Charles's lips on his. But he heard the lorry far behind them start to speed up.

He had to get home and he had to warn his mother and sister.

That was going to be fun on its own. Not.

CHAPTER 13
21st September 2022
London, England

Jamie was absolutely furious with stupid pathetic MI5 or whatever security agency that idiot was with. How fucking dare they go after beautiful Luca. That was flat out outrageous and those agents involved in this conspiracy were going to pay dearly for this.

Jamie went straight into the jet-black headquarters of Division and sat on the very edge of rows of computers and desks and stared at the massive TV screen in front of him.

Maura, Harry and the Hill Twins stopped what they were doing on the computers behind him and all came around him.

Jamie loved them all but he was absolutely furious.

"They went after Luca. Alice is missing. I stopped an MI5 or whatever man tailing Luca," Jamie said.

Everyone tried to look surprised but they failed to hide their lack of it. Jamie wasn't exactly surprised himself. For the past two days they had been tracking the shipments of supplies Helen had bought and everything seemed to be moving into a warehouse owned by the Government in London.

The Hill Twins had managed to get Maura and Harry added to the warehouse's computer systems as security guards so they could just turn up to inspect the place tonight. Jamie was meant to join them but he just didn't feel comfortable leaving Luca.

"We need to solve this now," Jamie said.

"We needed to solve this last Friday," Maura said, gesturing the Hill Twins to do something.

It was then that Jamie realised each of the Twins had a sticky label on their red jumpers each with their own name on them. Clearly Maura had gotten annoyed at some point and made them reveal which twin was which.

Harriet grabbed a tablet and bought up on the TV everything they knew so far in order.

Jamie stood up perfectly straight. "The order's wrong. We don't need to work in the order we found the information. We need to work in the order Helen worked in,"

Everyone nodded and Harriet swiped at the tablet a few times.

Harry stepped forward. "On Helen's phone we recovered earlier emails that Maura's MI5 friend didn't have. We know the whole plot started back in

May when Maura started emailing an unknown person to see if the Government would unofficially back it,"

"Do we have any idea who she was emailing in May?" Jamie asked.

Maura sort of shook her head. "I've analysed the language and syntax of the email but it's government-style. It's cold, formal and like everyone else. It is probably the Prime Minister but I don't know,"

Jamie would have loved to deny that the Prime Minister couldn't do something so outrageously callous against his own people. But he would. And as the Prime Minister had said repeatedly peaceful Scottish nationalists were not his people.

"Then," Elena said," back Helen finally managed to get a confirmation from the mysterious emailer that the government would back it. Granted it still took Helen three weeks and constant emails to make it happen,"

"Helen started," Harriet said, "to meet daily with the Justice Sectary,"

"And that led to the release of the three terrorists, including David Fletcher," Jamie said.

Everyone nodded but Jamie could see the look of slight despair on everyone's faces. They had all worked in intelligence for so long but actually seeing your own Government willingly conspire to perform an attack was something else entirely.

"Then," Maura said, "in July the terrorists were released with a few complications that meant they were going back and forth to prison. They were officially released in the past few weeks,"

Jamie again hated the sound of this.

"What about these shipments?" Jamie asked. "When did they start?"

Harriet swiped a few times on the tablet. "There was a shipment of explosives and other things every single month on the second Monday since May,"

Jamie wasn't surprised. If he had learnt anything about Helen over the past few days it was that she knew exactly what to do. She probably knew for a fact the Government would unofficially endorse her little scheme sooner or later and then they would give her somewhere to store her supplies too.

"What about the meetings she had with the terrorists and corrupt Ministers over the weekend?" Jamie asked Maura.

Maura shrugged. "All gone dark. No social media. No phones. No one has seen them,"

Jamie didn't like the sound of this. It wasn't abnormal for Ministers not to turn up to work, it was just a way of life for a government, but these same people not turning up for work was troubling to say the least.

Jamie had to find out more. "Harriet can you ping Alice's phone please?"

Maura leant closer to Jamie. "Are you seeing him tonight?"

Jamie nodded like it was perfectly okay. To him it was.

"We need you with us tonight. We need another agent deary," Maura said.

Jamie knew she was probably right but he wanted to spend the night with Luca. He was so hot, beautiful and sexy that there was literally no one else he would rather be with tonight. And if some agency was targeting him then Jamie wanted to protect him.

"If someone is after him-" Jamie said.

"Then the best way to protect him deary is to go to the warehouse with us," Maura said coldly.

The Hill Twins and Harry went deadly silent.

"Jamie or Charles," Maura said. "I am happy for you but the mission comes first. The warehouse is filled with evidence. We need to scan it, get fingerprints and see how far up this goes,"

"And," Harry said, "we need to see how much explosives are there to determine the target,"

Jamie slowly nodded. They were both so right but he just wanted, needed to make sure beautiful Luca was okay.

"Guys," Harriet said loudly.

Jamie spun around.

"Monitoring Counter-Terrorism chatter and Alice has been arrested. They are moving her to a secure prison facility tomorrow," Harriet said.

Damn it. This was getting way too serious now.

"Counter-Terrorism is monitoring Luca's flat, phones and everything electronic, including the two people staying with him," Elena said.

This wasn't good in the slightest. They were

really going after Luca now and who the hell were the two people staying with him? Were they friends? Foes? Dangerous criminals?

Maura stomped her foot on the ground. "Damn them all. Jamie go to Luca. He must know something or at least have access to something. We all know intelligence agencies regardless of country don't focus this much on someone without good reason,"

Jamie wanted to point out this was a different case this time. These corrupt agents watching Luca just wanted to blame him probably for a terror attack but she was letting him see Luca.

He wasn't going to let her change her mind.

"Call me the second you're back," Jamie said demandingly.

"Of course," Harry and Maura said as they went over to the small gadget cabinet under the TV screen. "Time Set tonight is 11 o'clock. Three hours time,"

Jamie nodded. Time Set was always a scary concept for him, it meant if Harry and Maura didn't contact them by 11 then something had gone seriously wrong and then him and the Hill Twins needed to go dark.

He really wanted them to be okay but he doubted they would.

Division was fighting a massive enemy this time and they were completely alone.

That both excited and terrified him more than he ever wanted to admit.

CHAPTER 14
21st September 2022
London, England

Luca couldn't believe what the hell had just happened. MI5 or some agency was actually following him like he was some kind of terrorist. This wasn't happening, this couldn't be happening but it clearly was.

Luca had got into his apartment, and just fell onto the black very soft sofa and just closed his eyes. He was really glad both his beautiful sister Abbie and his mother Amelia were out shopping (and seemingly his cats were too) and said they would be back soon. Luca really hoped they wouldn't be back tonight actually whatsoever. Even more so if sexy Charles turned up.

Luca forced himself to sit up on his black sofa and there was just such a nice calmness about the living room of his apartment with his large TV on the wall surrounded by very full bookcases and a coffee table in front of him and the two great armchairs that faced each other on opposite ends of the coffee table.

When his mother and sister returned Luca had to tell them to be careful and that they were probably being watched, but he didn't want them to worry. He had never experienced this before, he actually had no idea what to do.

He just wished beautiful Charles would turn up soon.

Luca was actually a bit surprised Charles didn't beat him here as Luca had taken tons of shortcuts and diversions to get home so he had actually been gone for two hours.

Someone knocked on the door.

Luca felt his heart stop for a split second and he went over to the bookcase, picked up a massive book and slowly went out of the living room and into the hallway that led to the black front door.

Normally Luca didn't hesitate before opening the door because it was just that. A door. But tonight he hesitated, he didn't know who was there and he was scared if he spoke then the person would kick down the door.

"Hello can I help you?" Amelia said.

Oh shit. Luca had not wanted his mother and sister to come back this soon.

"I was meant to see Luca later," Charles said, his voice very unsure.

Luca couldn't blame him and now he really wished the ground could just swallow him up.

"We haven't seen many men lately. Have you banged yet?" Abbie said.

Luca seriously wanted to die about now.

"Nope. We've only kissed," Charles said.

"Excellent," Amelia said, clearly shaking her keys outside for some reason. "Better you test each other out first before you pop his cherry,"

Wow. Luca was probably going to need counselling about this.

Luca heard the key in the door's lock turn and before he could run the door opened.

Luca's mother, in a very flattering black dress that made her look even more amazing than she normally did, raced straight over to him and gave him a massive hug and kiss on the cheek.

Then Amelia picked up her shopping bags that Luca hadn't noticed she had bought in and went into the living room.

Abbie, who was about the same age as Luca, wearing some very heavy flowery perfume, jeans and a tank top just winked at Luca.

"They seem nice," Charles said, shutting the door and walking over to him.

Luca just hugged the amazing man he was really starting to fall in love with and kissed him on the cheek. He wanted to kiss him so much more but he wasn't in the mood yet.

"I'm sorry you have to meet them like this," Luca said. "They're staying with me for another two days,"

Charles smiled like it was nothing. "I'm here for

you. You're the only thing that matters to me,"

Luca felt a wave of emotion wash over him and he just led Charles into the living room, hand in hand.

"What's your name?" Abbie asked.

Luca was a little annoyed that the best women (only slightly ahead of Alice) had transformed his coffee table into a fashion show with all their *interesting* London clothes they had bought.

At least the two women were sitting in the armchairs opposite each other and Luca and Charles could have the sofa to themselves.

"I'm Charles Page," he said, sitting down next to Luca.

Amelia slowly nodded. "Not a bad name I suppose. You have a fit body so I could see why Luca liked you, but as I always said to your father, Luca, the only real test is to see what's in the underwear,"

Luca just rested his face in Charles's wonderful shoulders. He wasn't denying he didn't want to see Charles's body and wayward parts in their full glory, it just wasn't really something he wanted his mother to say.

"How did you meet?" Abbie asked, as she held up some kind of fishnet t-shirt or all-in-one shirt and trousers thing. Luca had no clue what it was.

Charles looked at Luca smiling. "We met at a party last Friday. This amazing man knocked into me when I was doing security work for the Met and I've been unable to stop thinking about him since,"

Luca loved that little confession and he

completely felt the same way, but his mother and sister focused on their clothes. His mother even held up a blood red dress that definitely couldn't fit her body shape.

"Where you are both from?" Charles asked. "Your accents say southern England but I'm getting a hint of Scotland too,"

Luca was impressed.

Still Abbie and Amelia started to talk about their dresses and clothes and whatever other crap they bought. All Luca wanted was to talk about how great Charles was but they clearly weren't that interested.

Charles leant behind Luca and kissed his neck close to his ear.

Luca gasped in pleasure.

"Have you told them what happened?" Charles asked.

"Nope but I will," Luca said.

"Now might be the best time," Charles said.

Luca wanted to argue and roll his eyes but he was seriously enjoying Charles's lips against his neck too much not to agree.

Luca pulled away and leant towards his sister and mother.

"I have something to tell you both," Luca said.

"Don't tell me you've already banged him so much. He's knocked the common sense out of you and you're done something stupid. He clearly isn't who he says he is," Amelia said.

Luca was shocked and was surprised Charles

looked so relaxed at the attack. Of course Charles was who he said he was and he was the only person willing to help him.

Luca at least needed to respect him a little for that, and trust him completely.

"Don't be silly," Luca said harshly. "We have a problem. MI5 have been following me and Alice is missing,"

"Actually," Charles said, "Alice has been arrested by Counter-Terrorism,"

Both women threw their clothes on the coffee table. Luca wasn't hopeful about their reactions to this sort of outrageous news.

"Damn the English. I like them but this is ridiculous," Abbie said. "I voted for Independence last time and I will again,"

Luca watched his mother only nod, clearly too annoyed to speak.

Abbie reached over and grabbed Luca's hand. Luca smiled as Charles looked like he forced himself not to protectively grab Luca.

"We must leave tonight then. We cannot stay in a country that doesn't like us. We must go back to Scotland tonight," Abbie said.

Luca seriously didn't want to point out how Scotland was still ruled by England and if MI5 wasn't concerned about arresting the First Minister on fake charges. Then Scotland definitely wasn't safer either.

It was probably more dangerous.

"Tell them all of it," Charles said.

Luca didn't like being backed into a corner but Charles did it with such love, respect and like he truly just wanted the best for Luca.

Luca rolled his eyes and told his sister and mother everything that had happened.

Abbie stood up and threw a shopping bag against a wall. It might have been filled with only clothes but Abbie had some power behind it judging by the bang it made.

"We vote for a Scottish Government that is ruled by an English Government. We pay tax that goes to the English. We live by laws set by the English and when we try to set our own, chances are the English deem them unlawful. What fucking more do these people want?" Abbie asked.

Luca just shrugged. There was nothing he could say about it.

Charles stood up and Luca forced himself not to smile like a schoolboy as he felt Charles playing with his hair.

"All we need to do is know that you're probably being watched," Charles said. "Me and some very secretive friends will try and stop it. I *will protect* you all,"

Luca felt an icy chill run up his spine. He definitely believed Charles at the end, he just didn't know why Charles was being so nice to him.

He hoped it was because Charles loved him but he wasn't sure.

"I'm going to bed. I need to think," Abbie said.

Then his mother followed.

Luca couldn't blame them.

But at least it was now him and Charles all alone in his living room together.

Without a single sister or parent or cat to disturb them.

Luca pulled Charles onto him and just let things happen.

And Charles didn't stop him.

CHAPTER 15
21ˢᵗ September 2022
London, England

As Jamie laid on Luca's large black sofa in his black boxers under a very fluffy black throw with Luca right next to him, he was completely amazed at what had just happened (or happened over the past two hours actually). Jamie was still stunned at just how amazing Luca was in every single part of his body and he was just such an amazing lover.

Jamie really hoped that this wouldn't be the only time they would have sex.

When Jamie had knocked on the apartment door and those two crazy ladies had come up to him, he had to admit he was concerned about Luca. He had thought that the two ladies were enemy MI5 and they were buying time whilst their friends hurt Luca inside.

It was only that he knew Luca involuntarily gasp inside that he didn't kick down the door. But the entire apartment was very nice. He loved the bookcases, the TV that sort of reminded him of Division HQ and it was so homey, something Jamie had never had or really wanted.

Until now.

Luca moved around a little bit and Jamie forced himself not to moan in pleasure for basically no reason.

Jamie knew fully well that they had only been dating for five days but he just felt like he had such a deep, loving connection with this beautiful man that he really wanted to spend the rest of his life with him.

"Want a drink?" Luca asked as he got off the sofa with nothing on and slid into some black boxers that really highlighted how great his ass was.

"No thanks," Jamie said as he watched Luca walk into the corridor with the front door that also probably connected to a kitchen.

Jamie reached over to the coffee table where his smartphone was resting and it was five minutes to 11.

Why the hell hadn't Harry, the Hill Twins or Maura called him?

This was a first in the history of Division as far as Jamie knew of including the decade he had worked with Maura at MI5 that she had been this late on a Time Set call. She never missed it. Hell no Intelligence Officer ever did.

That was how important they were.

Luca walked back into the living room with a small glass of deep red wine and Jamie just focused on his amazingly skinny beautiful body.

Then Luca sat on the floor, rested the back of his head on Jamie's six-pack and Jamie wrapped an arm round him. Luca kissed it.

"I'm sorry you had to be accused of being someone you aren't," Luca said.

Jamie seriously tried not to laugh.

He felt so, so guilty towards Luca. He had just had sex with an amazing man that he had been lying to the entire time and he was lying again. Literally straight after sex, surely that was immoral or just wrong?

"It's fine. It's clear they love you and just want to protect you," Jamie said.

Luca kissed Jamie's arm a few more times. "But that's why I have you,"

Jamie leant over and kissed Luca's soft lips again. And he just felt worse and worse about himself.

Normally he was perfectly okay with all the lies, deception and other immoral things he had to do on a mission. But this time it was so much harder and it felt like Jamie was destroying himself.

Jamie had had plenty of hot boyfriends before and he had lied to them about his work and felt fine about it. This time he felt like he was stabbing himself in the chest with each lie.

"What are you going to do about Alice?" Luca asked.

Jamie had a few ideas about getting her out but they weren't any ideas that a mere Met police officer could do. So yet again he had to lie to this sexy man.

"I'm good friends with the Met Police Commissioner so I'll ask him to write to the head of Counter-Terrorism for an explanation. And he will get some answers,"

Luca just sighed.

"But he's really good at his job and he'll ask to see the evidence. No actually I'll do one better for you I'll get him to take me to the Headquarters of Counter-Terrorism. That way they don't have time to make fake evidence,"

Luca slowly nodded and just started tracing little shapes on Jamie's arm. Jamie knew it wasn't the answer that Luca wanted but unless he told the truth Luca would have to accept this was beyond what a Met cop could do.

"What's the time?" Jamie asked.

Luca checked Jamie's phone and showed him it was 11 o'clock.

"You aren't leaving me right?" Luca asked.

Jamie laughed. "Of course not,"

All Jamie wanted to do at that moment was put on his clothes and run like hell out of the apartment. Clearly something massive had happened and this was not good in the slightest.

The operation had to be blown sky high for two agents like Harry and Maura to go dark or worse.

Jamie was going to have to slip out during the night and make sure that everything was okay. This wasn't a time for going dark.

Jamie's phone buzzed.

He tried to reach for it. Luca grabbed it and answered it.

Shit.

"Go Dark. Mission Blown. Maura, Harry captured. Jamie you need go dark. Shit. They're here," Jamie heard the Hill Twins say before screams filled the line.

Jamie snatched his phone off Luca and weakly smiled at him.

"What was that?" Luca asked like there was a possible explanation.

"He's not a Met Cop," Amelia said. Her and Abbie storming into the room.

Jamie just wanted to get out but he wanted to save his relationship with Luca if that was even possible.

"I have a friend in the Met," Amelia said, "he has never heard a Charles Page. He's fake,"

Jamie hated seeing Luca jump up and back away from him.

This was not what he wanted.

And he knew things were about to get even worse.

CHAPTER 16
21ˢᵗ September 2022
London, England

Luca had absolutely no idea what the hell was going on but all he knew with any certainty was that Charles or whatever his real name was, was not the man he fell in love with. All Luca had done was fall in love with a piece of fiction, a story, a lie.

He hated being lied to.

Luca went over and stood firmly with his mother and sister next to the bookcases that he treasured so much. And he just stared at Charles because he was a danger now to him and his family and quite frankly to the country he loved.

"What the hell was that?" Luca asked.

Luca was furious now. How the hell did Alice know that Charles was a liar, a cheater and just another Westminster pawn that wanted to stop his people's democracy.

He was stupid to believe in Charles. That was

never going to happen again.

"That was me trying to help you," Charles said. "My real name is Jamie, I work for a semi-autonomous agency for the UK Government. I am trying to help you,"

"Liar!" Luca shouted.

"Listen to me. The Government is planning an attack and will blame you for it. Me and my team were investigating and now something has happened,"

Luca stomped his foot on the ground. "You're lying. You're working with them. I trusted you. I fucking loved you!"

Luca hated seeing this dickhead in his living room just after they just had sex. What kind of guy lies to a man just to have sex? Charles or this Jamie man was clearly the worst of the worst.

"You're not listening to me," Jamie pleaded.

Luca didn't want to listen. He wanted to kick, scream and just wanted this dickhead out of this life.

He was done with English boys, he was done with all of this and he was certainly done with this cloak and dagger rubbish.

Luca threw his arms up into the air and pushed his mother and sister out of the way. He stomped into the corridor that led to the front door and he just hoped that Jamie would get the hell out.

How could Luca be so stupid and vulnerable. He wasn't a spy. He wasn't a man. He was just some pathetic gay boy from Scotland trying to believe that where he came from didn't matter in this city and country.

Maybe all the bullies, ex-boyfriends and everyone who was ever nasty to him was right. He didn't belong in England, he was just a weak, pathetic queer boy that didn't deserve anything in life.

Luca was so mad with the world right now. He wasn't even sure he was actually mad at this Jamie guy, but his betrayal and lies and deception only bought back all the hate he had been running away from for years.

He actually never wanted to go to university to become a doctor first of all. He wanted to become an actor (something he had mentioned in private to Charles... no *Jamie* in passing). Luca only became a psychologist to prove to the bullies they were all wrong about him.

A few moments later he saw Jamie being dragged out of the apartment by Amelia and she punched him as he was thrown out.

Weirdly enough Luca had the urge to go and make sure he was okay. But Luca was so done with that dickhead.

Their entire relationship was based on a lie and he hated Jamie for it.

Luca hated himself even more for falling for a lie.

CHAPTER 17
21st September 2022
London, England

Jamie's face pulsed with pain as he was thrown out of beautiful Luca's apartment.

Jamie felt so defeated that he simply sat outside the large black front door on the cold concrete floor that formed the corridor where the rich wealthy apartment owners lived with the normally very nice floor-to-ceiling windows with stunning views of London behind him.

In all honesty he hardly would have cared too much if the window his back was resting on cracked and collapsed.

At least he wouldn't feel so bad about himself. All he had been trying to do was simply protect that cute sweet little man that he was head over heels in love with.

On all his missions, travels and adventures, Jamie had never met such a hot man that was also so sweet, loving and he actually felt like he could have a connection with. When they were having sex, Jamie couldn't help but imagine spending their lives together, telling Luca about his real job and traveling the world together (with Jamie doing missions there in secret).

It was such a little fantasy but it had honestly felt like it could truly happen this time with this amazing man.

Jamie huffed as that was never ever going to happen. And he had screwed up not only the relationship he really wanted more than anything else in the entire universe, but he had screwed up his protection detail.

Now MI5 and whatever other corrupt agency could come for Luca and his family with nothing stopping them. Jamie couldn't believe how much danger he had put them in now all because of that phone call.

The phone call.

Jamie shot up and started to walk down the corridor checking his phone.

There were messages and pings from intelligence agencies saying what he had feared. A mysterious woman and elderly man had been captured in a warehouse, and two identical twins had been captured in an unknown terrorist hideout.

Jamie quickly checked another Division Computer system and thankfully the Hill Twins had activated the protocols for these sort of situations.

Jamie put his phone back in his pocket, and thankfully right now thousands upon thousands of fake information and fake news was being pumped from servers all over the globe into the UK's intelligence networks. It would take the Secret Services days, if not weeks, to find out who Maura, Harry and the Hill Twins actually were.

Especially as each piece of fake information confirmed five others but contradicted thousands more. Jamie didn't feel sorry for whoever had to sort out that jigsaw puzzle of truth and lies.

But this didn't exactly help Jamie right now. He needed to focus on finding the truth, he knew that Helen was probably behind all of this but she would have ordered (illegally) Alice to be arrested.

That was the key.

Jamie couldn't understand why Helen had been so careless to actually arrest a very powerful Scottish politician. Alice had to be the answer to everything.

Then it hit Jamie.

It made perfect sense really. Jamie knew that Helen planned to use Alice as the terrorist that would kill the idea of Independence forever.

It made so much sense. Alice was the leader of the Scottish Government's Political Party, she was very close to the First Minister so everything would look like it had come from the top of the Scottish Government and Alice was hated by the English with a passion.

No one would dare to question the UK

Government's version of events and no English voter (which were sadly the only voter that mattered in UK Politics) would dare question the Government if they stormed into Scotland and killed every single Nationalist there was.

Regardless of how peaceful they were.

Jamie was about to turn a corner into another corridor with more great views of London when Helen Armstrong stepped out in front of him.

Jamie hated her black trench coat, long blond hair and black high heels. But she was alone. That was surprising.

"It's a shame isn't it you cannot find the right friends these days," Helen said, as she showed him security footage on her phone of all of Division in prison cells.

"You aren't going to arrest or kill me, are you?" Jamie asked.

"Of course not gay boy," Helen said. "You've been too busy with you queer friend to investigate me. I doubt you will become a challenge to me now,"

"Why?" Jamie asked as he felt Helen was about to walk away.

Helen smiled. "You're English so I'll explain it to you. The British Empire used to control a fucking third of the world, then the left-wingers and idiots destroyed it. We should have gone into those countries wanting independence and killed them all,"

Jamie shook his head.

"I am not," Helen said, "allowing England to

lose any more territory. *We* rule Scotland and if anyone wants to question that. Then they can argue with an English bullet,"

Jamie was just stunned into silence as he watched Helen walk away. Then his phone buzzed.

He got his phone out of his pocket and he seriously loved the Hill Twins. They must have added a new protocol that modified his smartphone into a Phone Cloner because Jamie's smartphone was now telling him he had completely cloned Helen's phone.

And she was getting a call now. Jamie listened to it.

"The gay's at the end of the corridor. Kill him. Don't kill his queer friend I need him," Helen said.

The bastard. *She* wasn't going to kill him.

Jamie had to get out now.

CHAPTER 18
25th September 2022
London, England

Luca was so glad that his amazing mother and sister had decided to stay with him for a few more days before they left tomorrow. Luca had just been so mad, angry and cold lately that he hadn't even wanted to leave his apartment much at all.

Why did he always have to pick the bad men? Why not for once couldn't men be hot, wonderful and actually good people?

Luca just laid on his black sofa in the middle of his living room with his coffee table holding the largest mug of coffee he could possibly find and his two armchairs were covered in interesting looking dresses that his sister and mother wanted to take back with them. Luca still hated the dresses but his family was being too wonderful to Luca for him to say anything.

His phone buzzed.

Luca just rolled his eyes. The last thing he wanted right now was for that liar jerk Jamie (or whatever his true name actually was) to be calling him. Luca hated him, Jamie was such an ass, liar and just a horrible person. Who knows how many people he'd killed over the years for the Government?

His phone buzzed again.

Then it dawned on Luca that it couldn't be Jamie because he had blocked his number after the first ten calls. So if he wasn't lying this time then Luca was sure that he could pull some government strings and unblock himself.

Spies were always so corrupt and immoral and dodgy people. Luca wished he had never ever met the jerk.

The phone buzzed again.

It was from a blocked number so Luca went to deny the call but he just accepted it without really knowing why.

"Luca?" Alice said.

Luca was so relieved to hear his best friend's amazing voice, but where had she been?

"Are you okay? I thought you were arrested by Counter-Terrorism on fake charges," Luca said quickly.

Alice took a deep breath down the phone and Luca couldn't pin what was wrong, but something was.

"Alice?" Luca asked.

Luca realised that the background noise was all

wrong, there was no noise, traffic or anything that was so typical of London's background noise that after a while everyone seem to tune out.

"I'm fine. I just… needed to have a few days away," Alice said.

"Without telling me or the First Minister," Luca said.

"Dearest Luca, you know I love you with all my heart, should we go out together on Friday?"

Luca absolutely knew something was wrong now. He had heard for years after a very messy drunk night that Alice would have loved him not to be gay but she never would have said it like that, to his face without alcohol in her.

This whole conversation was fake but Luca just knew he needed to play along.

"Of course I would like that," Luca said.

"Westminster Abbey on Friday…" Alice said. "Don't come Luca! It's a trap! Help!"

Someone hit the ground.

The line went dead.

Icy coldness shot through Luca as he realised that maybe Jamie wasn't such a jerk and a liar after all. He was definitely dodgy, untrustworthy and Luca was never going to sleep with him again, but maybe he had been right about the conspiracy.

And now they were trying to use Alice to get him to Westminster Abbey on Friday.

Luca had no idea why but he had to go and try to save his friend. It would make sense for the kidnappers to take her along anyway so Luca had to go and save her.

And he certainly didn't need some lying dickhead to save him.

Luca was just looking forward to Friday and it was going to be a tortuous week because of it.

And Luca was surprising himself with the things he did for the people he loved.

CHAPTER 19
26th September 2022
London, England

Jamie was absolutely amazed at the Hill Twins because he had no clue how they had managed to sort through 32% of Helen's phone in only two days.

Jamie had gone completely dark and off-grid for the past five days and was currently laying on a very lumpy hotel bed in some cheap bright yellow hotel room trying to sort through her phone. And it didn't help that Helen kept receiving phone calls.

"Where's Alice?" Helen asked through the phone call Jamie was playing.

Jamie just rolled his eyes as he hated being in such a small yellow hotel room that stunk of cheap beer, sweat and condoms. He didn't know who had used the room last but they certainly didn't clean up properly, and the hotel owner hadn't either.

"She's safe. She will be converted very soon," a man Jamie didn't know said.

"That doesn't matter. Just kill her at the event on Friday and make it plausible she built the bombs," Helen said.

Jamie almost cheered to himself as Helen had finally, after five long days, made a slip on the phone call. So he was looking for a major event on Friday, probably evening that Alice was going to attack.

Jamie searched his laptop and cursed under his breath as there were literally thousands of political events going on Friday. From the UK Ambassador to Ukraine hosting a welcoming party for refugees to the Queen hosting something and thousands more.

It would be impossible to do a proper security scan and to check out every one of these venues. He had to narrow it down, Jamie just wished that beautiful Luca was here right now.

Jamie had no doubt that sexy man could help him figure out which target Helen would pick. It would have to be one that was important to the UK Government and would symbolise Scotland's enslavement to England.

That was probably how Helen would twist it in the media hence the reason for the targeting.

Jamie pretended to know a lot about Scottish history and politics most of the time but he wasn't an expert in the slightest. He knew the first Scottish massacre by the English had been something to do with King Edward the first somewhere in the 1200s or maybe 1300s.

But that was it.

Jamie quickly searched for when Edward the First invaded Scotland and it was 1296 but that didn't mean much. So for some reason Jamie decided to check where King Edward was buried.

He was buried in Westminster Abbey and that rang a bell for Jamie so he checked the list of political events going on on Friday.

There was only one happening at Westminster Abbey.

Jamie just shook his head. It was so clever of Helen to attack the very first (even though there were probably others) so-called Great Enemies of Scotland's resting place.

Jamie could see exactly how Helen could write the headlines now. *Pathetic Nationalist attack oldest enemy.* Jamie wasn't exactly a writer of headlines but he was getting concerned now

He had absolutely no backup. His friends were off-grid completely with the intelligence networks not revealing any single detail about their location, and the same went for Alice. Maybe they suspected Jamie was monitoring them but it wasn't helpful.

Jamie really needed Luca more than anything right now. He needed someone he could trust, know Luca would protect him and make sure that the attack didn't happen.

And most of all Jamie just wanted to tell Luca the truth. Not the half-truth, a spy's-truth or anything else. Just the whole messy chaotic truth about himself.

Jamie just hoped that Luca would still like and

maybe love him after that.

Another whiff of cheap beer kicked up in the room and Jamie just knew that he had to go to Westminster Abbey on Friday, five days away. The security would be too tight to get in before then so Jamie had to focus, study and make sure he was as prepared as he could for Friday.

And if he was killed on Friday by Helen's idiots then Jamie would be okay with that. He had lost Luca but Jamie wasn't going to let Luca live in a world where he would be imprisoned for peacefully wanting freedom.

That wasn't a world beautiful Luca deserved to live in.

CHAPTER 20
30th September 2022
London, England

Luca couldn't believe how many ugly old people were wearing disgusting ill-fitting black suits and dresses as he went into Westminster Abbey and stood to one side next to the grand archway that functioned as a posh door.

He wasn't a fan of the long Abbey with black benches and pews against the immensely tall walls, the horrible white and black square tiled flooring and the even so-called grander golden altar at the far end of the Abbey.

"Stay very still," a man said behind him with a harsh unloving voice.

Luca felt the icy coldness of a gun barrel being pressed into his lower back but he remained calm. As much as he hated Jamie or whatever his name was, he just knew that that was what he would do in this situation.

Luca absolutely despised the overwhelming aroma of coffee, cloves and cigar smoke that came from the man with the gun. He smelt disgusting but Luca didn't know how to escape.

"Do exactly as I say," the man said.

Luca didn't want to comply in the slightest. He wanted to kick, scream and run off to find Alice and save her. But Luca had very little doubt that these monsters had already spread lies about him through this crowd so they wouldn't believe him.

"The crowd," Luca muttered.

He wished he had been smart enough to see it earlier. He had just been so mad and outraged with Jamie's lies that he had failed to see why the enemy wanted him here in the first place. Luca recognised these people as judges, senior politicians from all sides of the political spectrum and some of the richest people in the country.

If Luca was going to bomb and kill a bunch of people, these would be the ones. And Luca had a sneaking suspicion that that was exactly why the bastard Helen had wanted him here.

And he had just walked into the trap.

A trap he now needed to escape from.

Luca slowly turned around, slightly surprised the idiot with the man didn't shoot him.

The idiot was exactly as Luca had imagined him to be from his voice

"You wouldn't shoot here. Not in front of your Masters," Luca said. "You wouldn't want the event shut down this early,"

The man grinned and Luca recognised him from pictures in newspapers in Scotland two years ago. This was David Fletcher's best friend, Gabriel Jackson, another terrorist.

Luca felt his skin go icy cold. He looked around but there was no one even looking at him, well there was three men but they didn't seem to care.

Gabriel gestured Luca to get moving by waving the gun subtly about.

Luca looked behind him and weighed up running but Gabriel jabbed him in the ribs with the gun.

"No running," he said.

A few people seemed to hear him but they didn't help. They simply moved away.

Luca stood firm and stared into Gabriel's eyes.

"I am not moving," Luca said loudly. "You can shoot me but I am not helping you kill these people,"

A few people looked again but none seemed interested.

Gabriel laughed. "So be it queer,"

Luca grabbed the gun. Gabriel seemed surprised.

Gabriel kicked him.

Luca hissed.

Gabriel whacked his fists into Luca.

Then Gabriel's body went limp and Luca gasped as he watched a man in a very tight sexy suit pretend to hug Gabriel like he was a little drunk.

The sexy man took Gabriel over like he was sleeping to a little chair right next to the archway door and he grabbed Luca.

Luca tried to resist but he focused on the sexy man's face.

It was Jamie.

Luca struggled, kicked and tried to escape. Jamie's grip tightened.

"Listen to me," Jamie said firmly. "There are bombs here. Alice and you are going to be framed for terrorism. Help me,"

Luca was sure he was lying, just spinning another web of deception, but there was just something so beautiful, pure and truthful in his eyes. That Luca knew he was telling the truth.

Maybe the first time in his entire life.

"Fine," Luca said bitterly. "Alice isn't up here. The idiot wanted to take me somewhere. Maybe the crypt,"

Jamie smiled and looked around.

"We go there then," Jamie said, offering Luca his hand.

Luca begrudgingly took it.

He had to save Alice, Scotland and his freedom.

Then he was done with Jamie.

CHAPTER 21
30th September 2022
London, England

Jamie was not messing around now. How dare these bastards threaten the man he loved and how dare they try to frame him for a terror attack.

Jamie stormed into the crypt that was made up of endless darkness with little pillars every metre or so that would give them absolutely no useful protection. Jamie wasn't even keen on the horrible ground, it was too smoothed and would create too many echoes to hide their movements.

Thankfully the ceiling was made up of little concrete domed features so at least that wouldn't create too much noise.

"Bombs armed," David Fletcher said in the darkness.

Jamie took out his gun with a silencer and beautiful Luca was behind him with a side piece that Jamie had given him on the way down.

Jamie took a few more steps into the crypt.

The lights exploded on. Blinding him.

"Drop the weapons," David said.

Jamie looked around and against the dirty white walls of the crypt was a guard dressed in military-issue body armour with a machine gun.

Then in each of the four corners of the crypt (which were definitely spread out a long ways) were four red flashing bombs. They were all armed. All ready to go.

"Bombs all armed sir," one of the men said to David.

Jamie focused his gun on David. Everyone laughed. Thankfully sexy Luca was too smart not to drop his weapon.

It was always a case of drop your weapon. Drop your life.

Jamie looked around. He needed something to distract the enemy so he could kill them.

Sadly there was David in front of him. Another guard behind him and another one each side of him. Four people to kill all armed with machine guns.

"What's the plan?" Luca asked.

Jamie loved that sexy man. He was buying him some time. But where was Alice?

Jamie couldn't focus on that right now. He had to focus on the bombs and sadly save the snobbish rich government upstairs.

"We knock you two out. We escape. We explode the bombs so when your bodies are found it looks like you were setting them and they went off before you could escape," David said.

Jamie hated these people but the bombs were the key. They were definitely made with C4 and that was Helen's mistake. The problem with C4 was that it was too stable.

Only a blasting cap could set it off.

Jamie aimed the bomb at the far left hand corner. He fired.

The bullet ripped into the bomb. The red flashing light stopped.

David screamed in anger.

Jamie spun around. Shooting the guard behind him.

The other people open fired.

Jamie tackled Luca to the ground.

He rolled off Luca.

Shooting one guard in the head.

Blood and brain matter splattered over the walls.

David and the last guard rushed over. Grabbing Luca. Putting him in a headlock. David gesturing he was going to snap Luca's neck.

The bastard.

Jamie rose up slowly and noticed that Luca was trying to fire his sidearm but it was definitely empty. It was amazingly hot that Luca had tried to protect him. He couldn't focus on that now.

"Drop your gun!" David shouted. His arm tightened around Luca's neck.

Jamie stood firm.

The last guard came over and took the gun from Jamie.

The guard wrapped his hands around Jamie's throat. He needed to escape. He couldn't save Luca.

He felt like a failure. He couldn't let Luca die.

Jamie struggled. Kicked. Screamed. He needed to protect Luca.

A gunshot went off.

Jamie's stomach twisted into agony. Luca couldn't be dead. Jamie struggled even more.

He could hardly breathe.

A blade shot out of the guard's mouth. His corpse slumped to the ground and Jamie took deep breaths.

Then he noticed that a very dirty looking Maura with a cut on her head and bruises on all over her arms stood right in front of him.

Jamie kissed her on the cheek and rushed over to Luca.

He was perfectly okay then stared with rage and hatred at David's corpse with his bleeding head making a mess of the crypt.

"You think really some English prison could hold me," Maura said.

Jamie smiled but he was more concerned and relieved that beautiful sexy Luca was okay.

Luca picked up David's machine gun and fired at the other bombs.

Jamie had completely forgotten about them for a moment. He was really glad that Luca was here.

"That's them done," Luca said.

Jamie quickly looked at them through the bright light that David had turned on and all four bombs were definitely destroyed.

But where was Alice?

And where was Helen?

Her plan had failed but Jamie knew that she was smart enough to have a backup plan.

Maura took out her smartphone. "Picked this up from a Division safehouse earlier. Pinging Helen's phone now,"

Jamie went over to Luca and held him tight. Thankfully he didn't resist and Jamie just loved him more than ever.

"Found her. Traveling in a car heading towards a private airfield," Maura said.

Jamie grabbed a few guns, Luca and started to race towards the stairs.

"Call every uncorrupt agent you know regardless of agency," Jamie said to Maura. "Get them to meet us at that field. This ends now,"

He had to stop Helen from escaping. She had to pay for all of this.

No matter what the law said.

FALLEN FOR A LIE

CHAPTER 22
30th September 2022
London, England

Luca really wasn't a fan of Jamie's driving as they zoomed across endless amounts of black tarmac in a black SUV they stole as they raced towards Helen's white bright jet ahead of them.

The white Land Rover Helen was in was driving at full speed towards the private jet.

Luca held onto the black door handles tightly as Jamie got faster and faster. The horrible private jet was sitting all by itself in a very open airfield. Their SUV and Helen's Land Rover were the only vehicles at the airport.

"Going to ram them," Jamie said.

Luca's knuckles turned white as he held on for dear life.

Their SUV got even faster and the Land Rover got closer and closer.

The SUV smashed into the Land Rover. Luca

screamed. The Land Rover was thrown off course.

It flipped into the air.

The Private Jet roared to life. It was preparing to leave.

Jamie smashed into the Land Rover again. Windows smashed and screams echoed around the airfield.

Jamie stopped the SUV. Luca got out and raised his sidearm towards the crashed Land Rover.

Luca watched Jamie get their first and drag a very battered Alice out of the wreckage.

Luca raced over to her and hugged her tight. It was amazing to have her safe and well again. He kissed her cheek.

Luca glanced over at Jamie to see he had dragged Helen in her blondness out of the car and he had pinned her against the car pointing his gun at her head.

He was going to kill her for no reason.

"You try to kill tens of innocent people. You try to blame two innocents for the attack. You tried to kill the man I love!" Jamie shouted.

Helen laughed. "You gay boys don't have it in you. You're just weak pathetic awful people. You are beneath people like me,"

Jamie looked like he was going to kill her.

Luca rushed over to him. "This isn't the way Jamie,"

Jamie seemed to hesitate at Luca using his real name.

Luca felt Alice protectively wrap her arms around him.

"If you kill her like this, you are just as bad as the English you were trying to stop," Luca said.

Helen laughed. "Pathetic Scots. You can kill me to prove you Scots are the best. There will be others. Maybe not as strong but Scotland will be enslaved again,"

Jamie stuck the gun into her mouth and his fingers tightened around the trigger.

"Jamie," Luca said carefully. "This entire fight and terror attack has been about stopping democracy and Scotland. Killing her in cold blood is not the Scottish way. She must face trial, justice and a jury. That is what is right,"

Jamie seemed to hesitate and Luca pulled away from Alice and gently ran his hand down Jamie's amazing back.

"Do not let her win," Luca said. "Let her face justice in Scotland and let's see how powerful she is in a real court of law, and she can finally see the truth, liberty and fairness that drives Scotland. Let her be shocked by the amazingness of it all and how different she is in a land that isn't so corrupt,"

Luca smiled as Jamie took the gun out of her mouth and simply hugged Luca. Luca buried his face into Jamie's wonderful neck and simply kissed him.

"Dumb queers-" Helen said before Luca whacked her in the nose.

The sound of police sirens filled the air and the

roar of helicopters overhead made Luca feel so relieved because it was all finally over and now Helen was done.

Well and truly done.

He had absolutely no idea how the hell news of this conspiracy would go down in England, Scotland and most importantly politically in Westminster. But Luca was definitely looking forward to going back to Scotland with Alice, a great place that he knew he was safe in and definitely loved.

As he finished hugging Jamie, Luca just stared at this hot beautiful man for a moment and as much as his lies, deception and secrets annoyed him. Luca had to admit that he loved Jamie, and he had gone above and beyond what a normal man would have done for him and his country and his friend.

Luca hooked an arm under Jamie's and they slowly started to walk towards a brand new SUV that Maura was standing in front of as (uncorrupt) Counter-Terrorism officers swarmed in and arrested Helen.

"I guess I should thank you," Luca said. "You did save me, my country and my friend,"

Jamie shrugged. "It is my job and I wanted to say I'm sorry for lying,"

Luca fully admitted it was a little awkward now because they had just stopped a massive conspiracy and Luca still wasn't too sure who Jamie was.

But he wanted to find out, that was for sure.

"So tell me beautiful," Luca said, "who is Jamie?

Jamie gave Luca a wonderful sexy laugh and kissed him quickly on the lips.

"Let me tell you a story of two different men from different countries who fell in love and you can tell me afterwards if you still want to explore what we have," Jamie said.

Luca liked his romantic style and he sort of guessed that whatever Jamie's *truth* was, he just knew that he was going to love, treasure and protect this amazing man for a wonderfully long time.

FALLEN FOR A LIE

CHAPTER 23
15th September 2023
Edinburgh, Scotland

Jamie and Luca both sat down on the cool, almost chilled, green grass in Edinburgh Park on a perfectly sunny day. Granted it might have been sunny, but it wasn't warm in the slightest, not that Jamie minded.

He loved Edinburgh Park, especially sitting on the wonderfully sloped side of a hill covered in grand tall oak trees with crisp leaves in a rainbow of reds, browns and yellows that seemed to welcome in the autumn seamlessly.

Jamie loved the view from the sloped hill even more with him being able to see the great stone towers of breathtaking Edinburgh castle that stood like a proud watchman over the city and Scotland alike, and behind Jamie and the hill was a beautiful river and even more delightful trees.

Edinburgh Park really was a wonderful sanctuary

in the middle of a thriving capital city.

As beautiful sexy Luca rested his head on Jamie's shoulder, Jamie gave him a kiss and really savoured the softness of Luca's hair and just everything about him.

The sheer crispness of the refreshing cool air seemed like it was trying to seep the stress of the past year out of Jamie, but it sadly wasn't working, yet Jamie still wouldn't have the past year work out any other way.

As soon as Helen had been arrested, him and Luca and Maura had set to work freeing the rest of the team, which ended up with some blackmailing and threatening to various heads of organisations. So thankfully it didn't take too long for the Hill Twins and Harry to be freed, then with the UK Government and even the media of all things deciding to play down the deaths of 3 former terrorists (the third one had been hiding as one of the guards that Jamie had killed in the crypt) and the arrest of Helen Armstrong and several other Government Ministers.

Jamie had decided to go nuclear. He had convinced (a strong word for simply asking) Harry to give the Hill Twins permission to leak everything they had uncovered about the conspiracy to the press.

Harry had jumped at the chance so Jamie leaked it all and Alice and the First Minister of Scotland had been very grateful for the information. So whilst they jumped on the airwaves in Scotland, Jamie and Maura subtly convinced different English media outlets to jump on the story.

It didn't take as much convincing as Jamie feared.

Within days, the story was spreading like wildfire and whilst every other English person in the country and on TV said they didn't like the Scottish for wanting independence. They admitted the UK Government went too far this time.

But the UK Government had ordered no one to be arrested and charged and tried for the conspiracy.

Even now Jamie was hardly impressed with the Government for taking that line, but they were as corrupt as they come.

Thankfully after the Hill Twins commented on a few posts people started protesting, and Jamie was just shocked at how peaceful and massive that protesting got. There was even one day where London was so packed full of protesters that the entire city was close to collapse.

No police cars, no vehicles at all and no trains could operate because no one could get to work. There were just so many protesters.

But the Government held on.

As Jamie kissed Luca again as they both sat in wonderfully peaceful Edinburgh Park he honestly didn't know that most of the past year had been just as hard as trying to stop the conspiracy in the first place, but that was why he was so glad to have his amazing sensational Luca at his side.

Jamie was really shocked back in January (after two months of fierce protesting against the UK

Government) Alice had come to Division handing over the *Security Files* the Scottish Government kept to stop the UK invading them outright and it had worked as a failsafe for over a century.

Yet when Jamie was reading them he was amazed at all the things he had no idea went on over the decades. Some of it was just headshaking, and yet Alice had wanted them to release it all (as long as her name was kept out of it) to add even more pressure to the protesting.

So Division did.

Jamie just smiled to himself as he gently pulled Luca onto him as they both laid down on the wonderfully cool grass, just relaxing and actually taking a moment to focus on themselves after the past year.

Thankfully with even more blackmail material unleashed against the UK Government, the protesting intensified, all opposition parties in the UK parliament refused to attend any meetings until the ruling party resigned and then every single worker in the public sector went on strike to.

The entire country had so little police, ambulances and other public sector workers that the country actually suffered a blackout for two days. Mainly because there were no National Grid workers to fix the fault.

Then the entire UK Government resigned and then the intelligence agencies descended upon them like vultures ready to feed.

Jamie watched a very strangely shaped cloud as he gently ran his fingers through Luca's perfectly soft lifeful hair, and he absolutely knew he was the luckiest man in the entire world to be laying in a park with such a beautiful man, just like how normal people did.

That was definitely a nice change, just being normal for a moment, and not spies.

After the UK Government resigned in January, the country actually improved and there wasn't as much chaos as everyone feared there would be (because the UK hadn't had a government since the conspiracy was first revealed in September to be honest) and there was a general election, a new government got elected and then that was where things really got interesting.

The very last thing Jamie had ever expected to happen was the new government had gave Scotland a brand new Independence Referendum, something every single UK political party promised in the election they would deny, and even the result shocked Jamie, and even Luca who supported it completely.

Over 75% of Scots voted to become independent.

All the experts, Alice and Luca had repeatedly told Jamie, it would most probably be in the low 50%, but clearly a lot of Scots were a lot more annoyed at the conspiracy than they let on. And Jamie couldn't blame them, why the hell would they want to be ruled by a government (that they didn't elect) that was prepared to frame them for terror attacks?

It made no sense.

Jamie looked at wonderful Luca as he rolled onto his side and just stared at Jamie, and Jamie seriously loved staring into Luca's amazing sapphire eyes that really did look like priceless jewels.

Because Luca was priceless.

Luca gently kissed Jamie again and again and Jamie grabbed his hand, and felt their wedding rings knock together.

That was definitely been a sensational surprise to Jamie, he hadn't even expected Luca to ask him to marry him as soon as the result of the Referendum had been announced, but as Luca had said to Jamie, *there's no one else I want to enjoy my freedom with.*

And as Jamie hugged his new husband in their new city in their newly freed country, Jamie still couldn't believe how lucky he had been, and now he was definitely looking forward to an amazing future with the man he loved.

"Come on love birds," Maura said. "There's work to be done,"

Jamie looked up and just smiled as he saw Maura, Harry and the Hill Twins standing there firmly excited about getting to work.

Scotland might not have been part of the UK anymore but that was all part of the fun, because Division lived on, and Jamie was really excited about working with his amazing husband, team and country solving impossible problems.

The future was bright and amazing and filled

with possibilities just as Jamie liked it.

GET YOUR FREE AND EXCLUSIVE SHORT STORY NOW! LEARN ABOUT NEMESIO'S PAST!

https://www.subscribepage.com/fireheart

Keep up to date with exclusive deals on Connor Whiteley's Books, as well as the latest news about new releases and so much more!

Sign up for the Grab a Book and Chill Monthly newsletter, and you'll get one **FREE** ebook just for signing up: Agents of The Emperor Collection.

Sign Up Now!

https://dl.bookfunnel.com/f4p5xkprbk

About the author:

Connor Whiteley is the author of over 60 books in the sci-fi fantasy, nonfiction psychology and books for writer's genre and he is a Human Branding Speaker and Consultant.

He is a passionate warhammer 40,000 reader, psychology student and author.

Who narrates his own audiobooks and he hosts The Psychology World Podcast.

All whilst studying Psychology at the University of Kent, England.

Also, he was a former Explorer Scout where he gave a speech to the Maltese President in August 2018 and he attended Prince Charles' 70th Birthday Party at Buckingham Palace in May 2018.

Plus, he is a self-confessed coffee lover!

OTHER SHORT STORIES BY CONNOR WHITELEY

Mystery Short Stories:

A Smokey Way To Go

A Spicy Way To GO

A Marketing Way To Go

A Missing Way To Go

A Showering Way To Go

Poison In The Candy Cane

Christmas Innocence

You Better Watch Out

Christmas Theft

Trouble In Christmas

Smell of The Lake

Problem In A Car

Theft, Past and Team

Embezzler In The Room

A Strange Way To Go

A Horrible Way To Go

Ann Awful Way To Go

An Old Way To Go

A Fishy Way To Go

A Pointy Way To Go

A High Way To Go

A Fiery Way To Go

A Glassy Way To Go

A Chocolatey Way To Go

Kendra Detective Mystery Collection Volume 1
Kendra Detective Mystery Collection Volume 2
Stealing A Chance At Freedom
Glassblowing and Death
Theft of Independence
Cookie Thief
Marble Thief
Book Thief
Art Thief
Mated At The Morgue
The Big Five Whoopee Moments
Stealing An Election
Mystery Short Story Collection Volume 1
Mystery Short Story Collection Volume 2

<u>Science Fiction Short Stories:</u>
Gummy Bear Detective
The Candy Detective
What Candies Fear
The Blurred Image
Shattered Legions
The First Rememberer
Life of A Rememberer
System of Wonder
Lifesaver

Remarkable Way She Died
The Interrogation of Annabella Stormic
Blade of The Emperor
Arbiter's Truth
Computation of Battle
Old One's Wrath
Puppets and Masters
Ship of Plague
Interrogation
Edge of Failure
One Way Choice
Acceptable Losses
Balance of Power
Good Idea At The Time
Escape Plan
Escape In The Hesitation
Inspiration In Need
Singing Warriors
Knowledge is Power
Killer of Polluters
Climate of Death
The Family Mailing Affair
Defining Criminality
The Martian Affair
A Cheating Affair
The Little Café Affair
Mountain of Death

Prisoner's Fight
Claws of Death
Bitter Air
Honey Hunt
Blade On A Train

<u>Fantasy Short Stories:</u>
City of Snow
City of Light
City of Vengeance
Dragons, Goats and Kingdom
Smog The Pathetic Dragon
Don't Go In The Shed
The Tomato Saver
The Remarkable Way She Died
The Bloodied Rose
Asmodia's Wrath
Heart of A Killer
Emissary of Blood
Dragon Coins
Dragon Tea
Dragon Rider
Sacrifice of the Soul
Heart of The Flesheater
Heart of The Regent
Heart of The Standing
Feline of The Lost

Heart of The Story
City of Fire
Awaiting Death

Other books by Connor Whiteley:

Bettie English Private Eye Series
A Very Private Woman
The Russian Case
A Very Urgent Matter
A Case Most Personal
Trains, Scots and Private Eyes
The Federation Protects

The Fireheart Fantasy Series
Heart of Fire
Heart of Lies
Heart of Prophecy
Heart of Bones
Heart of Fate

City of Assassins (Urban Fantasy)
City of Death
City of Marytrs
City of Pleasure
City of Power

Agents of The Emperor
Return of The Ancient Ones
Vigilance
Angels of Fire
Kingmaker

The Garro Series- Fantasy/Sci-fi
GARRO: GALAXY'S END
GARRO: RISE OF THE ORDER
GARRO: END TIMES
GARRO: SHORT STORIES
GARRO: COLLECTION
GARRO: HERESY
GARRO: FAITHLESS
GARRO: DESTROYER OF WORLDS
GARRO: COLLECTIONS BOOK 4-6
GARRO: MISTRESS OF BLOOD
GARRO: BEACON OF HOPE
GARRO: END OF DAYS

Winter Series- Fantasy Trilogy Books
WINTER'S COMING
WINTER'S HUNT
WINTER'S REVENGE
WINTER'S DISSENSION

Miscellaneous:
RETURN
FREEDOM
SALVATION
Reflection of Mount Flame
The Masked One

The Great Deer

Gay Romance Novellas
Breaking, Nursing, Repiaring A Broken Heart
Jacob And Daniel
Fallen For A Lie

All books in 'An Introductory Series':
BIOLOGICAL PSYCHOLOGY 3RD EDITION
COGNITIVE PSYCHOLOGY THIRD EDITION
SOCIAL PSYCHOLOGY- 3RD EDITION
ABNORMAL PSYCHOLOGY 3RD EDITION
PSYCHOLOGY OF RELATIONSHIPS- 3RD EDITION
DEVELOPMENTAL PSYCHOLOGY 3RD EDITION
HEALTH PSYCHOLOGY
RESEARCH IN PSYCHOLOGY
A GUIDE TO MENTAL HEALTH AND TREATMENT AROUND THE WORLD- A GLOBAL LOOK AT DEPRESSION
FORENSIC PSYCHOLOGY
THE FORENSIC PSYCHOLOGY OF THEFT, BURGLARY AND OTHER

CRIMES AGAINST PROPERTY
CRIMINAL PROFILING: A FORENSIC PSYCHOLOGY GUIDE TO FBI PROFILING AND GEOGRAPHICAL AND STATISTICAL PROFILING.
CLINICAL PSYCHOLOGY
FORMULATION IN PSYCHOTHERAPY
PERSONALITY PSYCHOLOGY AND INDIVIDUAL DIFFERENCES
CLINICAL PSYCHOLOGY REFLECTIONS VOLUME 1
CLINICAL PSYCHOLOGY REFLECTIONS VOLUME 2
CULT PSYCHOLOGY
Police Psychology

A Psychology Student's Guide To University
How Does University Work?
A Student's Guide To University And Learning
University Mental Health and Mindset

www.ingramcontent.com/pod-product-compliance
Lightning Source LLC
LaVergne TN
LVHW011836060526
838200LV00053B/4064